T0243890

ZAPWIRED

A NOVEL BY
HAL ROSS

TITLETOWN
PUBLISHING

TitleTown Publishing, LLC
P.O. Box 12093 Green Bay, WI 54307-12093
920.737.8051 | titletownpublishing.com

Publisher: Tracy C. Ertl
Editor: Cliff Carle
Designer: Erika L. Block
Production Manager: Lori A. Preuss

Names: Ross, Hal, author.
Title: Zapwired : a novel / Hal Ross.
Description: Green Bay, WI : TitleTown Publishing, LLC, [2023] |
Originally published as "The Deadliest Game" (TitleTown, 2013).

Identifiers: ISBN: 978-1-955047-13-5 | 978-1-955047-16-6 (eBook)

Subjects: LCSH: Video games--Fiction. | Terrorism--Fiction. | Mass
               murder--Fiction. | Kidnapping-- Fiction. | Fathers and
               daughters--Fiction. | BISAC: FICTION / Thrillers / Terrorism. |
               FICTION / Thrillers / Technological.

Classification: LCC: PR9199.3.R598 Z35 2023 | DDC: 813/.6--dc23

For Sylvia and Barry

PROLOGUE

Khalid Yassin sat behind the wheel of his Lincoln MKZ in bumper-to-bumper traffic on the Triborough Bridge, relieved that his wait was almost at an end. A full year of living in New York among the infidels was hard to take. Plotting. Organizing. Ensuring that nothing was left to chance.

He was a tall man in his early forties, his dark brown hair combed neatly, sunglasses shading his eyes. Of mixed blood, he had refined features and a lighter skin color that enabled him to easily pass for an average American, adapting various aliases whenever necessary.

He reached his Long Island destination forty-five minutes later. A dirt road led past a vacant farmhouse to a large gated property. Several posted signs warned that the area was private and that trespassers would be prosecuted. Security cameras were locked in place. He pressed a remote switch on his sun visor and the gate slowly opened, then automatically closed behind him.

Yassin drove for nearly a quarter of a mile before reaching the entrance to what appeared to be an old country estate. Off in the distance sat a sprawling, three-story house. There was no view of a major road—just row upon row of pine trees, sufficiently mature to block the view. There was no barn or stable, only the house and a deserted guard station, with a tan Ford sedan parked next to it.

He pulled up alongside, shut off the motor and took a small package out of the glove compartment. It had arrived this morning via courier. Yassin was anxious to see if what he'd been told about its contents was true.

When he opened his car door and stepped out, he was greeted by Abdul Masri, his second in command. Abdul was close to his own age, though his thick black beard was speckled prematurely with gray. He wore a robe and kaffiyeh.

"*Asalaam aleikum.*"

"*Waleikum asalam,*" Yassin replied.

They embraced like brothers, kissing each other on both cheeks, then patting shoulders before moving apart.

"Is everything prepared?" Yassin asked.

Masri nodded. "Precisely as you instructed."

Yassin was about to hand over the package when he winced. Damn shrapnel injury, suffered years ago while on a clandestine excursion into Israel. Too often he forgot that certain movements caused the pain in his upper arm to flare. He rubbed the sore by habit, but it didn't help.

Masri took the package from him, opened it, and removed a metal cylinder, ¼ inch in diameter and 1 inch in length. "Please wait here," he said.

*

Ten minutes later Masri returned. Yassin could hear cries for help coming from the house. Masri speed-dialed a number on his cell phone. The explosion that followed was controlled, yet fierce. There was a brief flash of light, but only in one room—in the left corner of the top floor.

Yassin was thrilled. This new hybrid of C-4 plastique, NC-5, was sufficiently pliable to be hidden in a tiny space, yet powerful enough to cause the damage he wanted.

He followed Masri to the house. Although the lighting was dim, Yassin could still see signs of decay: patches of rust around the kitchen sink, brown floral wallpaper peeling, doors hanging off their hinges and tilted at odd angles. The staircase they took was splintered, making the climb precarious.

A skylight in the ceiling helped brighten the top floor. The two men passed a bathroom, two bedrooms, then paused at a third.

Yassin opened the door and smiled at the sight of the remains of the victim: a middle-aged vagrant Masri had abducted off the street two days ago. All that was left of him were his feet, resting where he'd been tied to a now destroyed chair.

Yassin shivered with excitement. Once more he was reminded of his loss and his vow to exact revenge. In his mind's eye he visualized thousands of victims, American infidels all. He could see them comfortably seated in their family rooms, gathered around the TV. Then, *BAM!* Their bodies ripped apart, the walls and ceiling stained with brain matter, bits of bone and flesh scattered everywhere; the smell of blood, distinct and metallic in nature, permeating the room.

What a sight to behold!

PART ONE
MAY

1

I was in my Manhattan office preparing to tackle a huge stack of paperwork when I heard scuffling outside my closed door. Before I could get to my feet, Nora, my secretary, came bursting in.

"I'm so sorry, Blair. There's a gentleman here who insists on seeing you. I told him he needs to make an appointment, but—"

I sat in awe as the man pushed his way past her and plopped down into the chair facing my desk.

"Sir!" Nora gasped in frustration.

"It's okay, Nora. I'll handle it."

I waited for her to leave before turning to the intruder. "You are?" I asked, looking at him warily.

"John Dalton." His eyes were cold, dark orbs.

"What do you want?" I said, wishing I'd sounded more authoritative.

"Five minutes of your time," Dalton intoned, his baritone voice projecting the same chill as his eyes.

"Sorry." I indicated the stack of files on my desk. "I can't even spare a minute."

The man's smile looked disingenuous. "Relax, relax. I was told you guys in the toy business were a fun-loving bunch."

"Oh, we are," I countered dryly. "It's a barrel of laughs here in Toyland. Now, what's so important that you had to bull your way in here?"

"Oh, c'mon, Anderson. Are you always this uptight?"

I wondered how he knew my name, but didn't bother to ask. I just wanted him out of here, ASAP. _

Again, I gestured at the files. "Either I get through this today, or I'll be swamped all day tomorrow. *Capische*?"

"I can see you're busy," Dalton said, though it was clear that he couldn't care less. "But your government needs you." He removed a laminated card from his wallet and handed it to me, seemingly oblivious of his clichéd words.

There was a federal seal and a color photo of the agent, bearing enough of a likeness to point out his arrogance.

"BIS," he said, as if that explained everything; then translated: "Bureau of International Security. We're an elite division, not well known, and that's the way we like to keep it."

"So, what do you want?" I demanded.

Dalton appeared to be about five years older than me, which would peg him at forty-two. He was powerfully built—over 6 feet tall and around 180 pounds. His hair was thick and dark. He was wearing a heavy worsted wool suit and a topcoat. Not the most comfortable clothes for a warm spring day in New York.

The black attaché case he was digging into resembled a computer bag. Dalton removed a 5 x 7 color photograph and passed it to me.

I blinked in recognition, unable to hide my surprise.

"Jeremy Samson," Dalton said, as if the man in the picture needed an introduction.

Jeremy and I were not only business associates, but friends. I couldn't for the life of me figure out what he was involved in that might affect me.

"You and Mr. Samson meet in Tel Aviv two or three times a year," the agent continued. "He oversees the distribution of a number of your products—not only in Israel, but across the Middle East. One of the manufacturers Mr. Samson uses is connected to an unsavory faction. As a matter of fact, ever since 9/11..."

"Wait a minute!" I slapped my desk with the palm of my hand. The mere thought of my friend being connected to something "unsavory" was impossible to swallow.

"Cute kid," Dalton said out of the blue, his eyes now focused on the framed photograph next to my computer, a 6 x 9 color snapshot of Sandra, my six-year-old pride and joy.

I took my daughter's picture and placed it flat on my desk.

Dalton's expression returned to dead serious. "As I started to say, Mr. Anderson, ever since September 11, we've become far more vigilant about American businesses being conducted in foreign countries. And you're in a position to do your government quite a bit of good."

I decided to humor him for the moment. "What exactly does Big Brother expect of me?"

"You'll be going to Israel in two months' time, correct?"

"So?"

"So, we need you to move up the date of your trip and do something for us."

I stiffened. "How do you know where I'll be traveling to? And when?"

"We're the government, Mr. Anderson. We—"

"I know, I know," I finished his sentence. "You know everything."

"Precisely. So, hear me out. As a Canadian enjoying the

benefits of living and working in the good old U.S.A., I'm sure you would be more than happy to cooperate."

There was something in the agent's voice I hadn't noticed before, a slight accent of some sort, but I couldn't identify it.

"A short while ago," Dalton continued, "while conducting covert operations, we happened upon a document that caused us to doubt the squeaky-clean reputation of a company you've been dealing with. We believe SDC—Seligman Daniel Corporation—is involved in money laundering that aids a faction connected to terrorism. By associating with this company, Jeremy Samson is involved, even though it might be inadvertently. All we need you to do is to convince your friend to switch production from this manufacturer to another. A simple task, really. And of course, we'll compensate you for your time."

I shook my head. "Jeremy's one of the most honest people I know. And he's thorough. He would've checked the company out. If there was even a hint that something was improper, he'd have dropped them. Look, I appreciate your concerns, but I'm afraid you're targeting the wrong guy." I stood and held out my hand.

Dalton ignored it. Rising, he said, "There's no mistake, Mr. Anderson. Jeremy Samson may not be aware of what's going on, but we can't overlook the facts. I guess I haven't made myself clear: Your government isn't asking—we're *telling* you. You're the only one who can influence Mr. Samson's decision. So, we need your help. If you refuse, I can promise, that secret project you're working on—Zapwired—will never see the light of day."

2

What the...? I was stunned. Zapwired was still in the R+D stage. No one, outside of a select group of people, was even aware of its existence. Once the product was released, I was certain it would totally revolutionize the gaming world.

However, I wanted Dalton out of my office, so instead of questioning him further, I gestured toward the door.

To my surprise, he flashed a cocksure smile, turned, and left.

Dalton had not only put me off balance, he now had me worried that the most important release in my company's history could be in jeopardy.

My mind churning, I looked out the window. The view from the 20th floor of Thirty-Seventh Street west of Eighth Avenue wasn't glamorous. But I'd chosen the location for the affordable rent, rather than to impress anyone.

I left my office and headed down the corridor to our showroom. The toy samples inhabited more than a thousand square feet of space—from board games to radio-control cars to talking dolls—95% of them with electronic components.

I'd made it to New York, despite my less than affluent background. After high school, I'd worked weekends and nights to pay for college in Montreal. Then, degree in hand from McGill University, I'd begun a career in computer sales. I moved into toys after a chance meeting with a distributor in Toronto who needed someone to fill a senior position.

It turned out to be a perfect fit for both parties. The business grew quickly in size and profitability. One particular firm we represented featured a diverse product range. The owner was an aging New York entrepreneur anxious to bring in someone young and hungry enough to manage and eventually take over the company.

When his offer came, my boss at the time encouraged me to go for it. A week of discussions led to an opportunity I never thought I'd find. And here I was, ten years later, president and owner of AT&E, short for American Toys and Electronics.

But success did little to bolster my ego. I seldom deluded myself: What had gotten me here was my ability to stay on top of things, always paying attention to the smallest detail. What motivated me was my constant fear of returning to the poverty of my youth if my business should fail.

*

Everything I sold was proprietary. A quarter of our products were created internally, while the majority was licensed from some of the leading design houses in the industry. Royalty payments approached hundreds of thousands of dollars per year—and life was good.

But recently, my company—like many others in toys—found itself in a financial bind. Phthalates topped the list of plastic ingredients considered hazardous to a child's health. As were magnets. And even the tiniest percentage of lead in paint. Enhanced testing procedures became necessary, but this resulted in an extra cost for the manufacturer.

Simultaneously, the working conditions of the labor force in China were now vastly improved, with far more costly compensation put in play. Over 3,000 toy factories had either been shut down or voluntarily gone out of business, enabling those that remained to demand huge increases for the goods they produced.

The toy industry worldwide had always submitted to the most intense scrutiny. And I was in favor of safety first. However, I was irritated by the fact that many major retailers revamped their own testing procedures, then demanded that toy manufacturers absorb this prohibitive expense.

They also applauded the changes in China, were vocal about workers getting a better shake, but refused to accept price increases on the goods they purchased.

This meant that the middlemen—distributors like me— had to take the financial hit. If it were a case of my own ineptitude, at least I could say I tried, but failed. However, it rankled to see my livelihood jeopardized by both manufacturers and retailers, who were only concerned about what was best for them. Realizing there was nothing I could do about it just added to my ongoing frustration with this aspect of the business.

*

I approached a locked cabinet in the near corner of the showroom, opened it with a key I kept on me at all times, and removed a Styrofoam-encased package.

Only one thing could save my company from slipping into irreversible debt. One product, actually. And I was convinced that this was it.

While many of my competitors boasted about America's Silicon Valley, or how brilliant the Japanese or Germans were, often it was some high-tech company in Israel that was a creator or partner in developing whatever technology happened to be *du jour*. If I'd learned anything—thanks to my friendship with Jeremy Samson—it was to always take the Israelis' talent and ingenuity seriously.

Because of them, I now believed I had a unique opportunity. Most who worked in my business harbored the desire to come up with the next big thing, *the* one toy that could take the world by storm. Much of our product was a crapshoot, unfortunately, with fickle consumers and an even more fickle group of retailers.

This craving for the "big score" ran true in my industry largely because our products were ever-changing. Ninety percent of toys had a short lifespan; kids soon lost interest and begged their parents to buy them the next new thing.

I removed the Styrofoam, contemplated what I was holding in my hands, and felt goose bumps run up and down my arms. Every instinct, every bit of my experience, told me I was looking at the next craze, the next Xbox or Nintendo, *the* one product that would never get old. In fact, I believed that consumers would still be talking about Zapwired for years to come.

To be accepted as a partner in this venture, I'd invested most of the profit my company had earned since its inception. And Hillel Electronics was not easily convinced that they needed me—until Jeremy Samson pointed out the diversity of the toy market around the world, and that going it alone without an expert would be foolhardy on their part.

The product was lightweight and compact, only slightly larger than other portable units already on the market. Better still, it had a triple fold-out screen that offered a viewing space almost twice the size of its competitors. It used the latest micro module technology, in 3D, *without* the need for special glasses. Its colors were brilliant, and its memory capacity far surpassed the gigabytes of anything released to date. It also came in a case compact enough to be transportable, yet versatile enough to be used on TV screens, connecting wirelessly, in seconds.

My plan was to have it retail for the incredibly low price of $99, which meant very little profit. But I was using the printer/ink cartridge philosophy, knowing that the consumer would have to keep coming back for the "ink," which in this case were our mini modules, many of which took virtual reality to the next level. With a retail price of $30 apiece, each module was so unique I felt certain our potential audience would bite; and bite big.

Programming and graphics fed this part of the industry, and my partner, Hillel, was a pioneer in both. What mattered was that over $25 billion was spent on video games each year in the U.S. alone. Even a small share of that business would guarantee success.

*

I turned on the base unit and watched the screen come alive. There were mini joy pads built in and positioned on either side to accommodate the left-handed or ambidextrous player. The unit also boasted an above-average stereo speaker, plus an input jack for headphones.

I pressed PLAY and the module supplied with the unit flashed a rainbow of colors. Then the name leapt out, starting as a speck in the top left-hand corner, then building, building, building, until the entire screen was covered: ZAPWIRED.

I hit GAME SELECT and chose *Crossfire*, a one-person shooter game. I was immediately transported into a *Doom/Halo* scenario, with forces from the Dark Side preparing to attack innocent urban dwellers.

Once into it, the brilliant colors, superior graphics and 3D stood out. But what made it impossible to put down were the special effects, a never-before offered feature unique to our unit.

Get shot and the joy pad sent a *hmm-hmm-hmm* momentary dull ache through your fingers. Hit a villain and a simulated adrenalin rush traveled from your hand and along the skin of your arms, raising the hairs on end and bringing literal meaning to the "joy" pad. But accidentally shoot an innocent bystander and the "joy" turned to a "zap" of pain.

I imagined kids, as well as their college-age siblings—

and even their parents—getting instantly hooked.

"Hoo-boy!" I shouted as bullets came flying toward me. I began feeling silly after a while, blinking my eyes and dodging as best I could, but loving every pulsating minute of the sensation in my body when I actually *zapped* a bad guy.

3

My cell phone rang.

I glanced at CALLER I.D. and my face lit up. I shut the game down and answered with a terse, "Who dares to call me?"

"It's me, Daddy."

"Who?"

"Me. Sandra."

"I don't know any Sandra's."

"Yes, you do," she pleaded, laughing. "I'm your *daughter.*"

I purposely sighed. "Oh ... *that* Sandra."

We both giggled at our little joke. "What's up, kitten?"

"Did you remember this weekend?" she asked urgently.

I'd promised to take her to a carnival that was appearing in town for the next two weeks.

"Daddy?"

I visualized Sandra's beautiful blue eyes, a spitting image of her mother's, now my ex-wife. Both had curly blond hair, too. I pushed thoughts of my ex away and focused on my adorable daughter. "Sweetheart," I said, softly, "when it comes to you, I promise to keep my promise."

"Then we're still going?"

"Of course we are. What time did I say I'd pick you up?"

"Umm, I don't remember, Daddy. I think you said early."

"Good. Let's make it nine o'clock. But you can't stay up too late the night before, chasing the boys around the neighborhood."

My daughter's giggle turned into a belly laugh; a sound I loved to hear. "All right, Daddy. I won't chase the boys. I promise."

I hung up, was about to walk out of the showroom when a dark sense of unease flashed through me. I was certain it was connected to my daughter, but for the life of me, I couldn't quite grasp what it might mean.

4

Billie's Bar was located a few blocks from my office. Recessed spotlights in the ceiling angled away from the floor gave off a mellow glow. The seats resembled captains' chairs, each upholstered with a swivel-ability and a contour that was appealing, not only to the eye, but even an XXL butt. The music was eclectic and upbeat, varying from jazz to rock or pop, depending on the time of night.

It was a little after five p.m. when I arrived from work in my navy suit and red floral tie. I was the last of a dying breed of businessmen still semi-formally dressed.

I ordered my usual: a double Johnnie Walker Black, served in a highball glass with extra ice. Halfway through my drink, I reflected on how meek and indecisive I'd acted with John Dalton. But it was the story of my life. When I was growing up, I'd shared a two-bedroom rented flat with my parents and sister. My father was a competent carpenter but unskilled at business, a man who worked day and night to barely eke out a living. My mother worked in retail and also kept long hours. It was my sister—older by five years—who taught me her cardinal rules: Respect anyone in authority, pause before speaking, and turning the other cheek said more about a person than defending one's honor.

I wished I hadn't taken everything she'd said at face value; wished I'd grown up tougher and thought faster on my feet. I began to raise my glass in a toast to my mediocrity when I felt a tap on my shoulder.

Andrew Sciascia was my friend as well as my lawyer. His expertise was in family law, but he was well versed in other matters. I'd called him a few hours ago and explained that I needed his legal advice, and he'd agreed to meet me here.

Andrew was in his mid-forties, potbellied and balding. His mother was a clinical psychologist, his father a successful stock broker. One of four children, Andrew had grown up on Long Island in a privileged environment, with private schools the norm. He and I were from opposite backgrounds, yet became close friends after he handled my divorce.

I got the bartender's attention and ordered a Bacardi and Coke; Andrew's drink. When it arrived, my friend sat down and we toasted each other's health. Then I recounted John Dalton's drop-in visit.

"Don't I have any rights?" I asked. "He didn't request that I move up my trip to Israel—he *insisted* on it."

"Whoa! What agency does Dalton work for?"

"BIS. Ever hear of them?"

"Can't say that I have. Who are they?"

"He said it stood for Bureau of International Security. Apparently, it's an elite, secretive division of the U.S. government."

"What are you being asked to do? Be specific."

"You know my business associate, Jeremy Samson? Dalton claims he's unknowingly working with an Israeli company, Seligman Daniel Corporation. He says they're involved in money laundering to abet terrorists. I have a new product coming out called Zapwired that I'm staking my life on, and SDC is manufacturing it. Dalton wants me to move production elsewhere."

"So, what happens if you tell him no?"

"The guy didn't say exactly, but he insinuated that unless I cooperated, Zapwired would be stopped from its launch."

Andrew mulled this over, then said, "BIS, eh? I'll do a little digging. But would it do you any harm to move the production as requested?"

I didn't have to think about my answer. "It wouldn't be easy, but yes, it could be done. Though here's the thing: before you and I met, Uncle Sam gave me a real hard time about my Green Card. Caused me all sorts of aggravation. Even limited the number of days I could spend here in the States. So why should I cooperate with a secret agency of the U.S. government?"

"Okay, I get it. For now, stall them and let me see what I can find out."

"Hi, is that Andrew?" asked an attractive brunette who seemed to appear out of nowhere.

"Claire? What a surprise!"

I looked from one to the other, and could tell in a nanosecond that they were both putting on an act.

The woman was in her mid-thirties. The more I looked at her, the less attractive she was after my first impression. Her lips were puffy from Botox and her rose-colored sweater was at least a size too small. Her breasts stood unnaturally high and proud, two perfectly symmetrical cones, rock solid.

This was an obvious setup. I'd warned Andrew numerous times about trying to fix me up, but the guy just wouldn't listen.

"Claire, meet Blair," my friend said, emphasizing our names and chuckling at the rhyme. He then regaled the woman with my business prowess, most of which was exaggerated. "This guy took his company from nothing and turned it into a booming success," he concluded.

I was embarrassed. To change the subject the only thing I could come up with on the spur of the moment was to ask Claire what she did for a living.

"Guess," she said, her voice slightly nasal.

"I haven't a clue."

"Think about it," Andrew piped in, amused.

"Actress?"

"Uh-uh," she said.

"Lingerie model?"

Both laughed.

"Porn star?"

Their laughter exploded.

"Grade school teacher," Claire confessed, making it sound like I should've known.

I quickly finished my drink, then said, "You two have fun. I gotta go."

Andrew kept his silence, but his disapproval was registered by a slow shake of his head.

*

On the cab ride home, I thought about my hasty departure and regretted my rude behavior. But Andrew knew I hated being fixed up; that I wasn't ready for any more introductions.

In my one-bedroom condo, I made myself a grilled cheese sandwich, sat down at the kitchen table, and turned on my computer. I tried to Google Dalton's agency, but found nothing. I referenced U.S. government security agencies and got the FBI, the CIA, and Homeland Security. There was zilch on BIS.

What was it Dalton had said? *Not well known and that's the way we like to keep it.* I suspected that part was true. Up to a point. Few things were hidden from the internet. I believed there should be *something* on them. So why were they "invisible?"

5

Dalton's phone calls began the following morning and continued on and off for a day and a half. Then, my secretary walked into my office just after noon on Friday. Nora Kelly had been with me from the beginning. Brown hair and eyes, in her late thirties, her slender frame always too thin, she was easily rattled when the unexpected occurred. Yet, she was so efficient, I couldn't imagine being without her.

"I'm sorry, Mr. Anderson," she said. I can't stand it any longer."

"Why? What's happening?"

"That government guy doesn't let up. He's tried to reach you at least six times this morning alone."

"Look, the next time he calls, put him through."

Nora let out a sigh and left. I went back to work. I'd spoken to Andrew late yesterday afternoon. So far, he was unable to uncover anything on Dalton's agency. For the time being, I was on my own.

My phone buzzed and I lunged at the receiver. "Dalton! Dammit, why are you still bothering me?"

"*Shalom.*"

"Jeremy? *Shalom* to you, too. I ... was expecting someone else."

"Obviously. You in some sort of trouble, *boychick*?"

It wasn't the first time he'd used the Yiddish term—literally translated as "little boy". When I first heard it, I was sure he was insulting me, until he explained it was meant as a term of endearment.

"No, no," I said. "Nothing I can't handle. Where are you—your office?"

"Why not?"

"At 7:30 at night in Tel Aviv? How about having dinner with some gorgeous babe?"

Jeremy chuckled. "You know me—a workaholic."

"Sure you are. When there's no woman hanging onto your arm. What's up?"

"Well, speaking of women, this young lady I know is going to be in New York and I gave her your number. I hope you don't mind."

"As a matter of fact, I *do* mind," I sighed.

"Why? You can't keep sitting at home, pining for your ex."

"Pining?"

"Yeah. It means—"

"I know what it means, Jeremy. I'm not pining for anyone. I'm over Mandy."

"Good, so now it's time to start living again."

I pictured my friend in his office, curly red hair, sport shirt opened halfway down his chest, form-fitted to an athlete's body of just over six feet.

"I *am* living," I said half-heartedly. The truth was, I did miss having a woman in my life. But despite my friends' good intentions, I was sick and tired of their attempts to play matchmaker, like I was some shy, pimply-faced kid who couldn't find love on his own.

"Sure, you are," Jeremy said. "Listen, Blair, I told this girl you're not only handsome, but rich. She sort of likes that in a man."

"Uh-huh. I bet she does."

"Take her out. She's hot looking." He paused. "Promise?"

"Jeremy—"

"Promise?"

"Is this the only reason for your call?"

"Of course, it is."

"Don't have her contact me, Jeremy. I won't go out with her."

"Seriously?"

"Very serious."

*

The phone rang again not long afterwards.

"I need your answer," John Dalton said, as arrogant as ever.

"You were here only a few days ago," I protested.

"And I didn't say I'd wait forever," he shot back.

I gripped the receiver and kept quiet.

"Mr. Anderson?"

"Yes?"

"What's it going to be?"

"You need an answer today?"

"Right now. What we're asking is not unreasonable. Help us this one time and you'll never hear from us again."

I felt trapped. I wanted to say how much I resented his barging into my office, resented the fact that he accused my friend of being connected to something illegal.

"Well?"

The story of my life was acquiescing to the wants and needs of others. For once I wanted to take a stand, especially with this man whom I'd disliked at first glance.

"I don't have an answer *right now*," I said, and then surprised

myself by hanging up.

6

I was on my way to pick up my daughter, running late as usual, which was a bad habit that I knew I had to work on. Fresh Meadows in Queens hadn't been my primary choice for a home, but Mandy had insisted and I'd given in. Why sweat the small stuff? I'd reasoned. So, Mandy remained in the house she'd always wanted—a place where we and our daughter lived together for four years. And I became the owner of a bachelor pad on the Upper West Side.

Mandy had been working at a Saks perfume counter when I stopped in to purchase a gift for my sister. She wasn't tall, only five feet, but there was something about her that immediately drew me in. And it wasn't only the long blond hair or her expressive blue eyes. I liked the way she went about her sales pitch, smoothly convincing and not overbearing. I bought the selection she recommended, the latest from Givenchy, and the following day I went back for her phone number.

A week later, after only two dates, we were strolling through Central Park when she said, "Oh, look, the perfect spot."

Her "spot" was located behind a bridge embankment barely hidden from sight. She tugged until I joined her. The ground was hard and cold. I was uncomfortable as hell and was about to object when Mandy unzipped my pants. She pushed me flat on my back, then mounted me with such enthusiasm, I doubted I'd be able to last.

"Come with me!" she pleaded.

Similar trysts went on for months. The more exposed the location, the better. In the back row of movie theaters. In airplane restrooms. On the sand at a topless beach in Bali.

Mandy had one sister, Julia, who was three years younger. The girls had become close by necessity. Their father was prone to violence and their mother used the bottle as a crutch. Mandy protected her sister by attracting the physical abuse onto herself. In her teenage years, she began using boys to her advantage, most likely as a way to achieve a form of substitute revenge on the only male figure she'd had in her life. Normal sexual relationships were out of the question.

When Mandy announced she was pregnant, I panicked. I'd been seeking a way to break it off. The sex had been exciting, but I was too much of an introvert to ever be comfortable with it. Still, upon hearing the news about the baby, I agreed to Mandy's suggestion that we marry.

Sandra, however, was born not nine, but twelve months later, and the trap into which I'd been ensnared became obvious. But I lived with it; the love for my daughter overshadowing Mandy's machinations.

Soon we were celebrating Sandra's first birthday, then her second and third. Around the time Sandra turned four, Mandy began to go out with the "girls" on a regular basis. A few hours became four or five. Occasionally, she wouldn't come home at all. Whenever I questioned her, she'd always have a plausible excuse: She'd had too much to drink and crashed at a friend's house. Or they were singing at a karaoke club and she lost track of time.

For Sandra's sake, I was determined to keep our marriage together, though an inner voice kept telling me that I was being played for a fool.

In the end—ironically—it was Mandy who suggested I move out. The ensuing court battle shocked me. By some Machiavellian twist, I ended up losing custody of my daughter. My only salvation was that the judge granted liberal visitation rights.

*

I knocked and the door was opened, not by Mandy but by Joanne Morgan, the cleaning lady who'd been working for us every third Saturday, long before the divorce.

"Hello, Mr. Anderson. Mrs. Anderson tried to reach you. She and Sandra have gone away for the weekend."

"I beg your pardon?"

"She said she texted you."

I took out my phone and turned it on. I wasn't one of those fanatics who had to check it minute by minute for updates. Sure enough, there was a message from my ex:

SORRY FOR THE LATE NOTICE, BLAIR. FRANK INVITED US TO THE CATSKILLS. COULDN'T REFUSE THE CHANCE TO GET AWAY FOR A FEW DAYS. CALL ME.

Fucking Frank! I swore to myself. Mandy knew how much today meant to me.

I said goodbye to Joanne and waited until I was back in my 5-series Beemer before calling my ex-wife.

She picked up promptly. "Blair?"

"What kind of shit are you trying to pull? You knew about today! What I'd promised Sandra!"

"This came up at the last minute."

"So what? The proctologist says jump and you jump?"

"How many times do I have to tell you? Frank's not a proctologist." Her voice rose. "An ophthalmologist has nothing to do with your bum. Besides, Frank isn't like you, okay? He's ... considerate."

"Oh, yeah? How? By screwing you on the front porch so all the neighbors can watch?"

She disconnected.

I sat there with the phone in my hand, boiling with anger. I really didn't care what she did on her front porch. What rankled was that Mandy had probably lied to Sandra, telling her they were going to the Catskills with Frank because I'd called and canceled.

ר

Yassin walked proudly, close to a strut. He considered it his American Walk, his way of assimilating despite the hatred he felt for everyone who passed by him.

Today he was wearing Western-style clothes—jeans and a blue sport shirt. He turned west onto Forty-Seventh Street from Fifth Avenue and slowed his pace, strolling along the north side of the street.

He found it ironic to be here, on Diamond Jewelry Way, commonly known as the Diamond District. *Jew Way is more like it,* he was thinking. Everywhere he turned he spotted another one, with his *payot* slithering down his cheeks, and the *tzitzit* or fringes of his *talit* drooping beneath his black topcoat. They were old and middle-aged, a few in their twenties, each wearing either a yarmulke or an oversized black hat. Most carried a black bag or briefcase.

He could feel the hatred roiling in his gut. Millions of dollars were traded on this street every day, with millions in profit being earned by the very people he despised the most.

Look at them, he thought as he slowed his pace. *Look at their smug faces!* It galled him the way they went about their daily lives as if they were invincible.

Two Hassidic Jews in their mid-sixties were coming toward him now. He imagined what he'd do if he was back home, in Palestine. He'd pick up his pace and approach the men, wait until they were parallel to him, then jab an elbow into the one closest to him. The man would double over, an *oomph* escaping his lips. And then Yassin would take pleasure in shooting him, at point blank range, in the face.

How he wanted to act now, to vent his anger. But reason kept his violent impulses at bay. Vengeance on a massive scale was already being prepared, and he mustn't do anything foolish. Merely imagining the coming assault was as far as he could allow himself to go. He just had to hold on a short while longer.

He was fascinated by the shops on this street: display windows featured jewelry set with diamonds, from bracelets to earrings to necklaces. Many were extravagant; showy and ridiculous. Most of the shops were co-ops, with each counter serviced by an individual owner. Yassin acknowledged that not all were manned by Jews, but it made little difference. They were still Americans, weren't they? Heathens, the lot of them. Enemies of Allah.

*

He checked the address and stepped inside, almost blinded by counter after counter of glittering jewelry, resplendent under shimmering lights. He heard a mélange of voices, some raised adamantly in the throes of a sales pitch, others talking loudly on cell phones. He detected English, Russian, Yiddish ... and not surprisingly, various Arabic dialects. This particular building was owned by a sympathizer to the cause.

"Can I help you?" a middle-aged Iranian woman asked.

"Let me show you something nice," a tall, bearded man offered.

Yassin ignored the people who called out to him on his way through the store. When he reached the back, he stepped behind a tall divider and knocked on a door that was hidden from sight.

No response.

He knocked again.

Ibrihim Sala opened the door. He was in his late fifties, poorly groomed mustache and beard, hair mussed as if disturbed from sleep. No greeting; he just moved aside and beckoned Yassin to enter.

Once the door was closed, they embraced and bussed cheeks before holding each other at arms length.

"It's bin ... long," his host said in broken English.

Yassin became furious. Sala's eyes were drooping, his speech slurred. He'd known about the man's addiction, but had accepted his word that it was all in the past. Yassin swallowed his anger and asked how he was keeping.

"G...Good," Sala said haltingly. "Why not?"

"Impatient?"

"A—uh ... mostly. Is much longer?"

"Not much."

"Weeks?"

Yassin ignored the question. "Did you make the arrangements?"

There was no reply.

The room functioned as a small apartment, with a kitchen in one corner; a sofa, television and file cabinet in another. Walls were overpowered by photographs of imams or quotes from the Koran; some 8 x 10, others larger, all held in place by thumbtacks.

The men sat down next to each other on the sofa, a worn three-seater with weakened springs.

"I asked you about the arrangements," Yassin reminded his host.

"Would you like ... tea?"

Yassin glared at him. "How many people altogether?"

Sala hesitated as if not understanding the question. Then, brightening, he reported, "The—uh—eight for you asked. All ... naturalized Americans." He moved as if suddenly struck by a cattle prod, approached the file cabinet, rummaged through it, retrieved and handed over the list of names with their contact information.

Yassin gave it a cursory glance. "What's the split?"

"I think seven men ... one woman."

"You think?"

The man sat up straighter. "I ... *know*."

"And what exactly did you say to them?"

"Huh?"

Yassin touched the compact Glock in his jacket pocket, tempted to use it. "What did you say to the people you recruited?"

"W-What you told me say. That time would ... would not be their own. That no one can know ... what doing."

"And they accepted this?"

"Absolutely."

"You're sure?"

"Y-Yes. People ... like make money."

"Good," Yassin said, then glared at Sala. "I want you to listen very carefully, Ibrihim. You promised me you were clean, that you were off the meth."

"But..."

"Don't!" His voice was low yet menacing. "Do not test my patience. I was foolish enough to believe your lies. But no longer. You will get your coat and come with me."

"Now?"

Yassin stood. "Yes. Now."

"But, where going?"

Yassin knew where he'd like to go. Straight to the Hudson River, where he'd kill the idiot and dump his body. "I am taking you to see Abdul Masri," he said. "Now, move."

Yassin would allow his second in command to uncover what harm, if any, had been done. He'd also leave it up to Masri to decide Sala's fate.

8

Monday afternoon I picked up Sandra after school and drove her to a Baskin-Robbins close to her home, my way of making up for our no-go Saturday outing.

My daughter wasn't herself. We'd no sooner taken a seat when she turned to me and, with wide, innocent eyes, said, "Daddy—why do you hate Mommy?"

"Huh?" A freight train rumbled through my head. "I—uh—don't hate her. Why would you say that?"

She shrugged, her tiny shoulders practically swallowing her chin. "I don't know."

"Has Mommy told you that? Did she say I hate her?"

Another shrug. "If you don't hate her, why can't you live with us?"

I coughed a couple of times to consider my answer. "I would love to live with you, darling. But your mother and I don't get along."

"That's not what Mommy says."

"Oh? What *does* she say?"

"You should talk to her, Daddy."

*

After driving Sandra home, I thought about what she'd told me. Was it wishful thinking on her part, to have both her parents back together again? *Or was something else going on?*

Mandy was still managing the Givenchy counter at Saks. I reached out to her by phone first thing the following morning, asked if she and Sandra could join me for dinner.

"Why?" she said, a definite edge to her voice.

"Why not?"

"You mean, you have no reason? You just want to take us to dinner?"

"That's right."

"Blair..."

I didn't want to explain over the phone.

"What is it that you really want?" she probed.

"I said—"

"Yeah," she interrupted. "An innocent dinner, just the three of us. Well, why don't I bring Frank along? We can make it a foursome."

My anger rose. "I don't want the butt doctor's company."

"I told you—he's not a proctologist!"

"Oh, yeah, I keep forgetting. Anyway—can you make it or not?"

"I'll have to call you back. Give me a few days."

"No. I need an answer now, Mandy."

"*Christ!* Fine. This Thursday. Pick us up at six-thirty. And Blair—"

"What?"

"Don't be late. Okay?"

"Who, me?"

"Yeah, you. I mean it, Blair. I'm not going to wait around like the last time."

"The last time I had dinner with you and Sandra? What was I—fifteen minutes late?"

"Try almost an hour, mister!"

"Well, something came up at the office."

"That's exactly what I mean. Don't let anything come up. *Capische?*"

"Hey—that's my word."

"Yeah. Well, remember *my* words: "If you're late ... we'll be gone!"

9

I worked the rest of the day crunching potential Zapwired sales numbers, beginning with Abundant, the online retailer, then MyMart and Arrow. If I released too much product, I'd have a disaster on my hands. Stores would return unsold goods or demand a huge price break. If I misjudged and didn't ship enough, I'd lose out on profit. It was a precarious balancing act. My experience was all I had to reply upon. That, and a great deal of luck.

It was after seven by the time I left my office, and I was exhausted. A car horn beeped the minute I stepped onto the sidewalk. I believed it was for someone else and continued walking.

"Blair?"

I couldn't make out who it was—just a man in a Buick SUV. His hand beckoned me closer and I warily approached.

"Get in," John Dalton said. He was dressed casually in a dark-blue sport shirt, open at the collar, and navy pants.

I hesitated.

"Look—you either let me give you a lift home so we can talk, or I take you down to headquarters. What's it going to be?"

I reluctantly got in.

"Nice to see you again," the government agent said.

I realized he must've been waiting for me. "Keeping tabs on my whereabouts?" I asked as succinctly as I could manage, barely suppressing a snarl.

Dalton smiled. "You're valuable to us, Blair."

"Yeah. I'm sure I am. Well, I'm still thinking about it."

"There'll be no risk on your part. It's just a matter of following some simple instructions. Jeremy Samson won't even be aware that you're involved. As a sign of our appreciation, we'll deposit $50,000 into your bank account. I know you can use it. Your mortgage payments have been arriving late. Recently, child support was delayed. And your savings are practically nonexistent."

I turned to face him. Dalton was keeping his eyes on the road, but I sensed how pleased he was to have gleaned this much knowledge about my financial situation. "Let me off here."

"Here? On Tenth Avenue?"

"Yeah. Stop the car. I'd rather walk."

"Mr. Anderson—be reasonable." He kept driving.

*

Dalton dropped me off at my apartment after I agreed to give him my answer the next day. Before doing anything else, I called Andrew Sciascia at home and asked if he had a minute to talk.

"For you, of course," he said. "What's up?"

I related my conversation with the agent and mentioned that the pressure was getting to me.

"Don't let it," he advised. "Look—this isn't my domain, but the ball's in your court. You can win a case against the government if you have lots of patience. They can drag this out for many years and not break a sweat. The two things always on their side are time and money. They will *never* run out of either. Also, taking on the public government is different from taking on the private one. You can use the pressure of the press in the former; the press will be barred from all court hearings in the latter."

"Bottom line it for me, Andrew."

"Again, not my expertise. But in my personal opinion, if you can somehow convince the government that pressuring you will, in the end, be a waste of time, they might let it go. However, if they believe the stakes are high enough, they'll fight you tooth and nail for as long as it takes until you agree to cooperate."

I sighed. "So, I'm on my own?"

"More or less. Good luck. And let me know what you decide."

*

I came to work at 9:00 a.m. the following morning, picked up Dalton's business card and dialed his number.

"Blackwell Industrial." A female voice, businesslike, waited for me to speak.

Huh? I almost said aloud.

"Blackwell Industrial," she repeated.

"Yes—is John Dalton there, please?"

"One moment, sir."

I dangled the receiver in my hand.

"Hello?" Dalton greeted me in a casual tone.

"Mr. Dalton, did I hear the receptionist right? Who the heck is Blackwell Industrial?"

"That's our cover. Blackwell Industrial Solutions. Do you have your answer for me, Blair?"

I drew in my breath. The old me would've given in by now, especially with someone as demanding as this guy. But for once I wanted to do what was in my best interest, not someone else's. "I'm sorry," I said. "I still can't give you a definitive answer. I'll contact you when I can."

10

Thursday night, Mandy guided me toward the den in her home by beckoning with her index finger like a temptress, her pink blouse practically unbuttoned to her waist.

The house was different from what I remembered: Family photographs on the walls were replaced by abstract art. The kitchen and dining room were painted a light shade of taupe instead of the original white. Knickknacks were in abundance, including a jumbo papier-mâché image of Dora the Explorer.

Mandy proffered a glass of champagne, almost forcing it into my hand.

"Where's Sandra?" I asked, taking a seat on the leather couch.

"Why do you want to know?" came the coy reply as she sat down beside me.

"Mandy—"

"She's at a friend's house, sleeping over."

I put the champagne down on the coffee table and rose to leave.

Mandy playfully pushed me back and edged closer, placing her hand on my thigh.

"We were supposed to have dinner together," I reminded her.

"So?"

"The *three* of us."

She struck a pose, exaggerating her chest. "You mean, you'd prefer dinner over me?"

I laughed despite myself, then removed her hand and stood.

"Where are you going?" she said in a pouty voice.

I was halfway to the door when I turned. "Sandra implied that it was me who chose not to live with you. She even asked why I hate you. A six-year-old kid, for God's sake. What's the matter with you, Mandy? What the hell did you tell her?"

She rose from the couch and approached. "Is that what's got you so upset?" She went to put her arms around me.

I backed away. "I want you to stop feeding this crap to our daughter, Mandy. I mean it."

"Okay. I'll behave."

I waited.

"I will. I promise." She paused. "If you give us ... another chance."

I looked at her in surprise. "Huh?"

"Let's try again. Just a few dates to begin with."

"A few dates?"

"That's right."

"I don't think so." I'd learned my lesson. The two of us getting back together wasn't going to happen.

"Why not?"

"It wouldn't work."

"Yes, it would. You don't have anyone else in your life, do you?"

"What happened to your doctor friend? You dump him?"

"Not exactly."

The picture became clear. "He dumped you, then?" I turned for the door; opened it. "I guess you're never going to learn."

"What's that supposed to mean?"

"You figure it out," I said, and left.

11

I arrived at Heathrow Airport on Tuesday. My trip had been planned for months. Distoy was the U.K. version of the American Pre-Toy Fair, a vitally important show where manufacturers introduced new products to distributors from around the world. It was a popular way to gauge their reaction, to see what toys had the most potential for the following year.

My goal was not only to get feedback from buyers, but to actually pre-sell Zapwired to as many countries as possible. It was especially challenging because we intended to release Zapwired in August, a mere three months from now. Very few new product introductions were made on such short notice. It was anyone's guess if buyers would be willing to go against their normal way of doing business.

This year, Distoy was being held in May, one month earlier than usual because hotel availability for June was scarce. Apparently, two larger trade shows had booked the majority of space.

Now, my bags collected, I sat in a London cab stuck in traffic, giving me ample time to think about where the toy industry was headed.

It stung to realize that our business in America was imploding. The abrupt bankruptcy of Toys Galore had failed to warn retail leaders, especially MyMart and Arrow, that tough times might be ahead. Instead of taking a stand and becoming more aggressive by expanding their offerings, they carried on as always, risk averse, with profit margins remaining their prime motivating factor.

I hated to think where it might all lead.

As the cab neared Buckingham Palace, I once more admired the gold tint lining the top of the steel gate; the King's Guards in red tunics standing ramrod straight at each sentry post.

Within a few minutes, we pulled up at my hotel, The St. James Court. I counted out 75 pounds; the equivalent of $98 American.

When I stepped out of the taxi, a car directly behind drew my attention—a black Volvo with windows so darkly tinted it was impossible to see inside. I was sure it was the same car I'd spotted at the airport, a small decal of Big Ben attached to the bottom right corner of its windshield.

I took a step toward it. The Volvo pulled away with a squeal of tires.

Dalton again, I surmised, keeping me in his sights, no doubt.

*

I checked into Room 241 and picked up a dozen messages, mostly confirmations of preset appointments.

The larger manufacturers had booked all the suites in the hotel, so I had to compromise by using a regular bedroom and rearranging the furniture for my meetings.

A carton had been forwarded in advance of my arrival containing an early version of the box in which Zapwired would be packaged, along with promotional material. I'd transported the sample myself and unwrapped it with a combination of excitement and trepidation.

Right on time, there was a knock on my door. I opened it and said hello to Doug Flood, from the Australian company of Peacock and Lacey. Doug was a young-looking fifty, with the rugged features of an outdoorsman, from his unruly brown hair to his ruddy cheeks. I often teased him about his company's name, how it best suited a law firm.

"Hello, mate," he said, greeting me with a powerful handshake, his eyes alight with his usual charm. "Somethin' brilliant to show me, have you?"

Doug would be the first buyer to see Zapwired, so I was anxious. My choices were to demonstrate the product, pointing out its features and benefits—or say and do nothing. I chose the latter, handing the game to the buyer, and waited.

It didn't take long for Doug to get the hang of the game selection he tried. His eyes lit up each time he experienced the *jolt* of success or the *zap* of failure. After 15 minutes it became a struggle to get the console away from him. When I told him the low wholesale price, Doug immediately committed to 50,000 units for the Australian market.

And so it went for the rest of the day. Italy jumped in for 75,000, Spain for 55,000. Germany and France each bumped those figures up to 100,000 apiece. By the time cocktail-hour came around, I was finding it difficult to rein in my enthusiasm. Seldom had I met with such success on a new-to-market product. It seemed too good to be true. Which proved prophetic, as I discovered the following afternoon during my 4:00 p.m. meeting with J. P. Broley, my distributor in Great Britain and my last appointment of the day.

J. P. was in his late fifties with a full head of white hair and nearing retirement. No one knew what his initials stood for and he never told. His permanent scowl gave him a curmudgeonly look, while in fact, he was the opposite.

When I gave him the game, he went through the gyrations, playing with the unit and yelping out loud as the *jolts* and *zaps* took effect. I told him what his cost would be. Broley put the game down and slowly shook his head.

"I've seen almost the identical thing at this show from one of your competitors."

"What!" I said, stunned.

"Yes. Practically the same bloody product. And his price is twenty dollars less.

"Are you certain?"

"Positive." He searched through his briefcase and pulled out a business card. "Here—you can have this. I don't know this fellow from Adam, and I'm not sure I'd trust him. You should check him out for yourself. He's a few floors above you, in Room 541."

I took the card in hand: Simon Tractenberg–Ninth Wave Electronics. The company, like Hillel, was based in Israel, so the irony wasn't lost on me. But Zapwired was supposedly a proprietary product. Hillel held a registered patent on it. Jeremy had said so, and I believed him.

*

I was on the fly the moment Broley left my room, dashing along the corridor to the elevator, then up to the fifth floor. The toy industry was known for illegal knockoffs. This had to be another one. But the Distoy exhibitors like me worked by appointment only; there were no walk-ins and no exceptions. So, I'd have to think of a way to get into this guy's showroom.

I paused. Often, room service came by uninvited during the day to refresh the drinking water and ask if anything else was needed. I would use this now as my ruse.

I double-knocked on 541's door and called out, "Room Service," using my best imitation of a British accent. Nothing happened. I waited, then banged again, louder this time. Still no response. I returned to the elevator and rode to the lobby floor, where I made a beeline for Reception.

"Hello," I said to the attractive young woman behind the counter, "I'm Blair Anderson, here with the Distoy group," then lied: "I had an appointment with Simon Tractenberg of Ninth Wave Electronics in Room 541. But he isn't answering when I knock. Can you try that room for me?"

She turned away, typed on her computer keyboard, then immediately came back to me. "Sorry, Mr. Anderson, but Mr. Tractenberg has already checked out."

I thanked the woman and left, disappointed by the news. The length of the show was three days, with the first two being the most important, as this was when the "big" deals were usually consummated. Some exhibitors cut out the final day entirely. It was my bad luck that this guy had gone AWOL.

The minute I returned to my room I was on the phone to Israel.

"Who is he?" Jeremy asked.

I filled him in on the man's name, company, and his lowball price. "What's going on?" I asked.

He avoided my question. "I'll look into it, Blair. In the meantime, carry on as if nothing's happened. Did anyone object to our early release date?"

"No one."

"Are you getting commitments?"

"So far."

"Good. Keep it up. Call me when you return to New York."

I was reluctant to let my friend off the phone, certain he was holding something back. There were too many questions that needed to be answered.

"Blair—"

"Yeah. I'm here."

"Relax. I'll get to the bottom of this. Okay?"

"Okay." I slowly lowered the receiver.

*

I skipped dinner and was in bed before nine, but had trouble sleeping. The next morning, I went through my final appointments by rote. I kept waiting for someone else to mention the knock-off. No one did. At noon, I packed, checked out, and grabbed a taxi for the airport.

The spaciousness of London cabs was something I always appreciated. I told myself to follow the British example of a stiff upper lip. I'd faced hiccups before. I wondered how close to Zapwired Tractenberg's product really was, and how long it would take for things to play out.

Traffic ebbed and flowed. I was about to ask the driver if he could find another route when I did a double-take. The same black Volvo I'd recognized upon my arrival was just passing us on the right. I could no longer slough it off to coincidence. I was about to jot down the car's license plate, when my cell phone rang.

"How's London?" John Dalton asked.

12

I kept my eyes glued to the car. "Nice vehicle you have there, Dalton. Black matches your personality."

"Beg your pardon? What're you talking about?"

"Like—you don't know?"

"Know what?"

I placed my hand over the phone's mouthpiece and asked the driver to follow the Volvo that was now picking up speed.

"All right, governor," he said and stepped on it.

"Blair—"

I ignored Dalton's voice, watching as the black car sped around a bend. We made the same turn maybe 10 seconds later and as if by magic, the car had disappeared.

"Sorry, gov," the cab driver shrugged.

I turned my attention back to the phone. "Dalton—where are you?"

The sigh was pronounced. "My office in New York. What's going on, Blair?"

If Dalton was in his office, then who was in the Volvo? "I'll call you back," I said, knowing I had no intention of doing so.

*

We pulled up to the terminal fifteen minutes later. I paid the driver and was just stepping to the curb when my cell rang again.

"You didn't call back," Dalton growled.

I cursed modern technology. My connection to New York—or wherever the heck the government agent happened to be—was crystal clear. "Dalton—now what?"

"I thought we understood each other, Mr. Anderson. The U.S. government needs your help. This is a matter of national security."

"Still thinking."

"I'm afraid we can't wait any longer. You have two choices. Either book your flight yourself and give me the date, or tell me the date you'd prefer and I'll book it for you. I'll expect your answer this coming Monday." He disconnected.

13

The makeshift mosque in Brooklyn was located in the basement of a 3000 sq. ft. private home. Yassin lowered his forehead to the carpet until it touched.

Thirty minutes later, with the prayer service over, he was back upstairs putting on his shoes when a boy aged eleven or twelve, huddling with the Imam, drew his attention.

"Mohammad?" Yassin muttered beneath his breath. The resemblance to his dead son was uncanny. How could one boy look so much like another? *Or am I imagining it*, he wondered. *For the thousandth time?*

*

Yassin had been born in Palestine a year after his parents' marriage. His father had gone against custom by taking an outsider as his bride—a Christian from Norway, no less. She was a volunteer working for an obscure charity organization; one of dozens operating in Israel.

After Yassin's birth, people began to observe the lighter color of his skin and his other Scandinavian features. As he grew older, he was teased and harassed endlessly.

His mother insisted he learn to speak English and he spoke it well. This became a further black mark against him. On the other hand, his siblings, a boy and a girl born two and four years later—were spared the same fate, having inherited their father's physical appearance.

It took until his mid-teens for him to accept what Fate had bestowed upon him. By then, the embarrassment of his youth was tucked away and forgotten.

On his twentieth birthday, Yassin was introduced to a girl by a close friend of his. Madras was the most beautiful creature he'd ever set eyes upon. They began seeing each other, courting in public.

Sharia Law, which governed Muslim behavior, was not as restrictive as some believed when it came to what a couple should or shouldn't do. However, it was common practice for both sets of parents to approve their relationship, and in this case, they did. Just shy of six months later, they were married.

When Madras became pregnant, panic set in. As someone who'd lived with juvenile diabetes, she'd been told about the risks of having a child. Yassin pleaded with her to have an abortion. She refused, even though their religion made it clear that abortion was allowed if keeping the child might put the mother's life in jeopardy.

Their son, Mohammad, was born a month premature. Madras, as Yasin had feared, didn't survive the birth.

Yassin became moody and quarrelsome. The only thing that kept him from slipping further into depression was his son. As the boy aged, he began to resemble Madras more and more—with a pear-shaped face, thick eyebrows, and sensuous lips.

The two were rarely apart. Yassin taught his son how to play chess as well as soccer. He was surprised to see that the boy was not only intelligent but quick and agile on the field.

By the time Mohammad had reached his eleventh birthday, the Imam began taking an interest in him. Yassin found it an honor that his son was being asked to go on weekend retreats with some of the other boys.

While Mohammad was away, Yassin would use the time to study the Koran, to reflect on his life and try to make better sense of it.

Normally, by the end of the weekend, he'd anticipate his son's return … until one particular Sunday in March when a knock came on the door at 6:00 p.m., Mohammad's usual arrival time home.

However, instead of the Imam and his son, it was only the Imam standing there, pale, with a haunted expression on his face.

Yassin's breath caught in his throat. "Mohammad?"

"May I come in?" the Imam asked.

Yassin excused his rudeness, invited the man inside, and closed the door.

The Imam lowered his head slightly. "I am deeply saddened to have to tell you that it appears a missile struck the house where the seven students were staying." He removed a handkerchief and wiped his eyes. "They're gone, Khalid. Your Mohammad among them."

Yassin reared back in shock.

The Imam guided him to the couch in the living room and helped him sit. "I'm so sorry," he said. "Your son was one of the brightest boys it was my privilege to teach, eager to learn as much as he could about his heritage."

He paused when Yassin began to sob uncontrollably. He put an arm around Yassin's shoulder to assuage his grief as much as possible.

A couple of minutes later, the Imam continued, "Yesterday at noon I had an errand to run. I left lunch for the boys and was gone less than an hour. Upon my return, the house we'd been using for our retreats was gone, reduced to rubble, almost as if it had vanished. I could not believe what I was seeing. I left my car in the middle of the road and was charging toward the site when I was stopped by a policeman. I … I tried to fight him off. I was screaming by this time, repeating the names of the boys under my care. He wrapped his arms around me, then wrestled me to the ground."

Yassin's head threatened to burst. "H-How could this happen?" he managed to ask.

The Imam shook his head. "I don't know. I tried, but couldn't get the truth. A forensic team was sifting through the debris. This went on for hours, until it grew dark. The local Imam put me up for the night, then drove me back to the site this morning. Cadaver dogs were added to the search and almost all body parts that remained had been recovered and taken to the morgue.

"I came home a short time ago and have been going from house to house to explain to the parents what happened to their children."

Yassin had no memory of the Imam leaving. In his mind's eye, he continued visualizing Mohammad's body disintegrating into thin air.

He dragged himself into the bathroom, where he was violently sick. Afterwards, he washed his face with cold water and went to bed. But his sense of loss was so profound, sleep was out of the question.

At daybreak he was on his way to the area where the destroyed house had once stood. Tears involuntarily came to his eyes. He whispered his son's name beneath his breath. He knew he shouldn't linger but did so anyway, only leaving when a few of the forensic personnel still on the scene began eyeing him curiously.

He drove to the stationhouse. The policeman at the front desk immediately came to attention when he heard why he was there, and minutes later Yassin was seated in the sergeant's office.

He refused the offer of coffee. "I just need to know what happened," Yassin said. "Please. Who did this?"

The man was in his early thirties, broad-shouldered, with a deep, gravel voice.

"I am so sorry, Mr. Yassin." He struggled with a decision,

then finally said, "We've determined it was the Americans. Their missile was to have targeted the house next door to the one where your son was staying. It was rumored to be a safe house for terrorists, which wasn't true. Its most recent occupants were a schoolteacher and his family of four. But it has remained unoccupied for over a month."

He picked up a sheet of paper from his desk. "This is a press release issued by the Americans this morning. I'm not supposed to show this to any civilians, so please keep it to yourself."

Yassin took it in hand. The more he read the greater his hate for the perpetrators became. Instead of admitting their mistake, the Americans gloated about the mission being a strategic success, having eliminated known terrorists. They even called it, "A victory for democracy and the American way."

Yassin handed it back, then stood and left without saying another word.

His heart screamed for revenge. For the next few weeks, he did nothing but mope around the house. He didn't know many Americans, though he lumped them all in with the devil and he sought a retribution that would never be forgotten.

Finally, he paid a visit to the Imam. The men had bonded many years before, part of a group with secret forays into Tel Aviv, intent on creating havoc.

Yassin made it clear that it was impossible to sit still and do nothing.

The Imam heard him out, then said the timing couldn't have been better. He confessed to being involved in a side of Islam of which few who knew him were aware. "It's a well-financed group," he explained, "with millions of dollars at our disposal. We currently have a secret operation planned for North America. But the man I'd assigned to take the lead, Nassar Camir, has left too many doubts in my mind about his capability. How would you feel about replacing him? I need someone with a cool, methodical head. Someone who will act rationally at all times. Are you up to it?"

Yassin didn't hesitate. "It will be my honor."

They discussed the operation in more detail, then shook hands. The minute the Imam left, Yassin relaxed for the first time in days. This opportunity he was being offered was too good to be true. He swore to Allah that he would devote the rest of his life to making as many Americans as possible suffer a thousand-fold for the death of his son and the other boys.

*

He paused at the entrance to the house and waited for Abdul Masri to approach. The man was dressed in a gray sweatshirt and black slacks.

"Has the problem been rectified?" Yassin asked in Arabic.

"Without a hitch," Masri replied quietly so as not to be overheard. "Sala has been terminated. I found out that most of the people he recruited weren't vetted properly. They've been terminated as well. We have to start the process over again."

Yassin rocked back on his heels. *It's my own fault,* he was thinking, *for having blind faith in Sala.* "How long will this take?"

"Not long."

"There's little time left and no room for error, Abdul."

"I know that."

"Make sure everyone else knows it, too," Yassin warned.

14

I was back in New York fighting jetlag, awake on Saturday morning before 7:00 a.m., when I took a call from my daughter.

"D-Daddy? It's me."

"What's wrong, kitten?"

"N-Nothing."

"Are you sure? You don't sound like yourself."

"Can you keep a secret, Daddy?"

I wondered where this was going. "You can tell me anything."

"It's not good news."

God! I almost blurted aloud.

"I don't think I should be telling you." She hesitated. "Mommy said not to."

"Please, darling, I can't help you if you don't tell me."

Another long pause, then she said, "Mommy's taking me out of school!"

"Huh?"

"We're moving far away. To California. I ... I'll probably never see you again." She started to cry.

"Wait a minute, Sandra. Please. Don't be upset. How soon did your mother say this would happen?"

"Very soon."

"Today?"

"N-Not today." A hiccup in her voice.

"This week?"

"I ... don't know."

Mandy had been talking about the two of us getting back together, trying to make a go of it again. *Is this revenge,* I wondered, *because I'd said no?*

"Can you stop this, Daddy?"

"I'll do my very best."

"But what if Mommy won't listen?"

"Then I'll come visit you as often as possible."

"Will you?"

"I will. You can count on it."

"Even if we're a—uh—*bazillion* miles away?"

"Even then."

"Okay." Sandra's voice brightened. "I love you, Daddy."

15

My jetlag was pushed to the back burner as I fought to control my anger. *How can Mandy do this?* I asked myself. *Arbitrarily pull up stakes and move away?*

It was too early to call Andrew and I couldn't sit still. I grabbed my bag and headed off for a workout at the local gym. Despite the early hour, there were quite a few people already there; not one over the age of twenty-five.

It must've been my mood, because wherever I looked, I caught what seemed to be self-satisfied posturing. On the treadmill, elliptical cross trainer, and stationary bike. Men and women alike, some sweating profusely, some not at all. Most had pampered physiques that at another time I might have admired. Now, all I wanted to do was call them out for being narcissistic.

I kept exercising for a good hour, then went home where I showered and shaved. I hadn't had breakfast yet, so I soft-boiled an egg and gobbled it down with a single piece of toast. Hi-test coffee gave me new life. I checked the time and punched in Andrew's cell number on my house phone.

"How was your trip?" he asked.

I didn't want to get into the possible knockoff until Jeremy got back to me with some specifics, so I told him it went okay. "But there's something I need to ask you."

"What is it?"

I explained what my daughter had told me.

"Is the move set in stone," Andrew asked, "or was Sandra just guessing?"

"I don't know."

"How soon?"

"Another unknown."

"Well, you'd better talk to your ex, ASAP."

"I plan on doing that. But, in your opinion, where do I stand here?"

"You were granted liberal visiting rights. Mandy would have to clear this move with the court, most likely with the same judge who heard your divorce case. You talk to your ex and see if this is what she's really planning to do. If it is, I'll file a motion on your behalf to enjoin Mandy from leaving New York. Is there anything you've done that might sway the court's decision?"

"Noth—" I started to say, then stopped myself. "I was late on a recent child support payment. There was also a mix-up on a few others. But everything's up to date now."

"Talk to your ex and call me back. And Blair—"

"Yes?"

"Slow down, okay? You sound stressed out."

"I *am* stressed out! Christ, this is my daughter we're talking about."

*

I hung up and tried to reach Mandy. No answer at work or on her cell, so I left messages. I should've felt better after talking to Andrew but my anxiety wasn't abating one bit. What tumbled in my head was the old Peter Principal: If anything could go wrong, it would, and usually at the worst possible time.

I watched a little television, then began to read a novel by John Sandford. I dozed on and off. The time crept by. Evening approached and Mandy still hadn't gotten back to me.

16

I wasn't sure what brought me here, to Billie's. The walls started closing in on me at home, so I went out to grab a bite at a joint I frequented near my office. I was walking back and there was the bar. A voice in my head told me one drink wouldn't hurt.

My favorite establishment was quite different on the weekend from what it was like during the week. The businessmen had been replaced by couples and the odd single looking for a good time.

Unlike me, I was dressed casually in jeans and a sport shirt. My first drink of the night was a double Johnnie Walker Black. Before I could take a sip, I felt a tap on my shoulder.

"Excuse me, are you Richard?"

She was gorgeous and I figured it might be fun to pretend. I saluted her with my glass. "I am," I said.

"It's nice to finally meet you."

I couldn't look away. There was the silky blond hair, the shape of her dainty nose, her full lips. Even her style of clothes appealed to me—her red dress falling a few inches above the knee, a black belt pinching her waist. The only imperfection to be found was in her hazel eyes, the left being ever so slightly crossed.

"I loved your last e-mail," she said.

"Why, thank you."

"That's what attracted me to you."

"What? My salutation?"

"No, silly. The romantic in you."

"Oh—that."

"The way you write. With a poetic flair."

"'Jack and Jill went up the hill.'"

She laughed, then said point-blank, "You're not Richard, are you?"

"No," I shrugged, "but I'll be happy to keep pretending until the real Richard shows up."

She smiled.

"May I buy you a drink..." I waited.

"Lisa," she responded.

"Lisa—hold on." I signaled the bartender and he approached. I turned back to her. "What'll it be?"

"Fuzzy Navel, please."

The bartender nodded and started to prepare her drink.

I asked Lisa how she and Richard had connected.

"Through a dating site."

"So, why'd you think I was him?"

"His picture was far from a close-up. It was a he-man pose at the helm of a sailboat. 'Come sail away with me,' I think was the inference. Anyway, from what I could tell, he really looks like you."

"He does?"

"Yes. Five eleven. A hundred and seventy pounds."

"That *is* close. What else?"

"Dimples, actually."

"And…"

"The same build as yours." She paused. "What's your name, by the way?"

"Dick."

She burst out laughing. "C'mon now!"

"Blair." I tipped an imaginary hat.

"Blair—is it really Blair?"

"I swear on my firstborn."

"You … you're married?"

I shrugged. "Was."

"Why'd you split up?"

"Uh-uh. That's far too personal—and I hardly know you."

*

The more we drank the friendlier we became. I was sure Lisa wouldn't be able to keep up with me, but she did, never once saying she'd pass. It got to the point where I just had to nod at the bartender and our refills would magically appear.

Nearly 45 minutes had gone by and Richard was starting to look like a no-show. Fortunately for me, Lisa didn't seem to mind, claiming she'd give him an hour, tops.

"What d'ya do?" Lisa asked, now a slight slur to her words.

"I play with toys."

"No, seriously, Blair."

"I am serious. What do you do?"

"Masseuse."

"Oh yeah? In a m-massage parlor?"

She grinned. "Silly boy. I work for one of New York's top physiotherapists: Henry Fontaine. Ever … hear of him?"

For the first time I noticed the definition of her shoulders and arms. "No, can't say that I have. Is he well known?"

"Very. His clients include muh … members of the Mets, Yanks an' Rangers."

My eyes went wide. "No kidding?"

"I impressed you?"

"Yeah. *Wowzer!*" God, the drink was getting ahead of me.

"Well—" we both said at once.

Lisa looked at her wristwatch. "Hour's up."

"Game over," I quipped. "Looks like Richard's lost, eh?"

"Eh? Are you Canadian?"

I brushed an imaginary hair away from her forehead and kept her guessing. I really didn't want her to leave. I touched her glass. "Here's to poor Richard."

"Uh-uh," she objected.

"Uh-uh?"

"Here's t' us."

*

Brandt was Lisa's last name and she was an only child. She came from a working-class family, both parents born and raised in New York City. She was thirty, she said, but I found her demeanor to be that of someone older and wiser. There was a genteelness about her, something old-fashioned, yet refreshing.

I told her about the toy industry, how I'd started my career with a distributor in Canada, explained how I surprised myself, finding I had a knack for the product. "Stayed with the man for five years ... b-before opportunity presented in New York," I continued. "*And ... now I own the company.*"

"Are you good at what you do, Blair?"

"I made it in the 'Mean Apple,' didn't I?" I took her hand in mine.

"I like you," she said.

"I like you, too."

She covered my hand with hers. "Can we go somewhere quieter?"

I stood abruptly. "Thought ... you'd never ask."

When I stumbled, Lisa put her arm around me.

How much did I actually drink? I wondered, no longer able to feel my feet.

*

I know Lisa paid for the cab. But how we ended up in my condo was a mystery to me.

I actually liked the fact that she took charge, leading the way through the hallway, past the den and kitchen, into the master bedroom.

Conversation was moot at this point. She helped me off with my clothes and I flopped down on the still-made bed, belly first. Lisa said something about wanting to make me feel better. It seemed innocent enough ... until an iron-fisted set of knuckles began to knead my shoulders.

"Ow!" I called out, quickly sobering.

"Your muscles are tight."

"They are?"

"Yes. I've never seen anything like it."

"You haven't?"

"Not really."

"Ow!"

"Don't be a baby."

The pain was bringing tears to my eyes.

"This will do you some good," she promised. "It's therapeutic."

"It is?" I tried to distract her. "Lisa—"

She was humming to herself.

"Hey?"

"Yes, Blair?"

"Could you—uh—quit for a while? Let me catch my breath?"

"I will. Almost done..."

She dug in and I groaned.

"Feeling better?" she asked when she finally stopped.

"Oh, yeah," I gasped, the relief profound. "Much better."

"Perfect. Now—close your eyes."

"Huh?"

"Close your eyes and keep 'em closed."

There was a rustle of clothing. Then the warmest body imaginable was lying next to me.

I cheated and opened my eyes. Lisa wasn't quite naked, unfortunately. She still wore her bra and panties.

I went to kiss her.

She avoided me by pressing a gentle finger against my lips. "Sleep," she whispered.

I made a half-hearted grab for her breast.

She pushed my hand away ... gently. "Goodnight, Blair."

"But—"

"But, what?"

"Nothing. Goodnight, Lisa."

In the morning, she was gone.

יז

I stayed in bed longer than usual on Sunday, my head pounding from too much booze, my sore limbs reminding me of the so-called therapeutic massage.

I tried sitting up, felt a wave of nausea, slowly lay back down.

I thought of Lisa's hands kneading my flesh, her warm body lying next to mine, her slightly crossed eye.

Was it the left one, or right?

I couldn't recall. And why did it matter? For the first time since my divorce, I was attracted to someone. Call it unusual, call it chemistry, call it what you will....

Call it too much booze, a silent voice inside my head interrupted.

"No!" The word popped out of me like a shot. True enough, I'd had a lot to drink. But there was a connection there; I'd swear to it.

The urge to urinate was overpowering, so I stumbled out of bed and into the bathroom. Afterwards, holding onto the wall for support, I headed off in search of a note from Lisa. From the hallway throughout the house. No note. No business card. Nothing.

*

I went into the kitchen, made myself a coffee and sat down at the table. The phone caught my eye and I was reminded that I still hadn't heard from my ex-wife.

I tried her number at home; it went to voicemail. I called her cell. When she didn't pick up, I left a message, telling her it was urgent, and that she needed to call back.

My cell was lying next to the house phone. I turned it on and checked for messages; something I should have done first. There was just one from Andrew, asking if I'd heard from Mandy yet.

Then my phone buzzed while still in my hand. CALLER I.D. revealed a familiar Montreal number. I picked up before it rang twice.

"Happy Birthday, darling."

It hurt, hearing my mother slipping backwards again. "It's not my birthday, Mom."

"Yes, it is."

"No, it isn't."

"It *is*. I should know when you were born."

There was no point in arguing. My mother, barely into her seventies, had been suffering with Alzheimer's Disease for the better part of three years. It was distressing to hear her this way. There were still some lucid moments; but far too many, like now, where there was no talking sense to her.

I did everything I could to help financially. People who didn't know better raved about the Canadian medical system, not understanding that socialized medicine came with a hidden cost. Taxes in Canada were exorbitant, yet the caliber of healthcare was worsening annually. It often took months to see a general practitioner, let alone a specialist. And the system didn't cover private care facilities like the one my mother was in. The hefty monthly expense was taking a toll on my bank account.

"Are you planning to visit today?"

My mother, before the Alzheimer's, knew I lived and worked in New York. I had to tread lightly. "I can't today, Mother, dear. But I will soon."

Her tone became strident. "When? When will you come?"

"Soon, I promise." The last time I'd visited, a little over a month ago, she hadn't recognized me.

"Your father dropped in today. We had a lovely time together."

My dad died of cancer five years ago. "Mother—"

"Please? I'd really like to see you."

This was getting more and more difficult. "I'll come see you soon. Okay?"

Silence.

"Mother?"

From her sonorous breathing, I could tell she'd fallen asleep.

18

Monday morning at my office I was finally able to reach Mandy and asked what she was trying to pull.

"You going to lower your voice, or am I gonna hang up?"

"Sorry," I said, not aware I was fuming. "You're traumatizing our daughter, Mandy."

"Traumatizing our daughter? What are you talking about?"

"What've you been telling her?"

"Who—Sandra?"

"No. Kim Kardashian!"

"Frank's been offered a great job opportunity in California and asked us to move with him. I thought it would be a good change."

Change? "What does that mean? A change from what?"

There was no hesitation. "From everything. From you."

"Me?"

"Yes, you. And you're raising your voice again."

One minute my ex is trying to seduce me, the next she's following her boyfriend to the other side of the country. "I thought you said you and Frank broke up!"

"We did break up."

"And?"

"And now we're getting back together ... providing I'm willing to move with him to LA."

"This is not the best thing for Sandra," I said. "Besides, I have visiting rights. I won't let you do it."

"Oh, yeah? Let's see you try to stop me."

'Hey—I'm being reasonable here. *Capische?*"

"Sure you are. Well, you can stop playing tough guy, buster. I'll do what's best for me and *my* daughter. Whether you like it or not!"

And with that the connection was broken.

*

Dalton left a message for me at 5:30 that afternoon. Instead of calling him back right away, I reached out to Andrew.

"What's wrong now?" he asked.

"The friendly government agent expects my answer in the next few minutes. Help me out here, Andrew."

"If it were me, I wouldn't roll the dice."

"Enough with the metaphors."

"I'd cooperate. It's less of a risk factor. Maybe BIS can't stop Zapwired? Maybe they can? But why take that risk? And what if switching to another company turned out to be a good idea?"

*

I phoned Dalton and said, "I'm in."

"Fine," he replied. "I'll book your ticket soon as we hang up. First Class on El Al. Paid in full by Uncle Sam."

"Very generous of you."

"It *is*. We could be sending you coach."

"Oh, yeah? And I could change my mind and say I'm not going. What is it exactly you need me to do, Dalton?"

"Hillel Electronics, the company behind Zapwired, uses SDC as one of their primary manufacturing sources. We believe SDC has been corrupted. We need you to convince Jeremy that it would be in everyone's interest if he talked Hillel into switching production from SDC to a company called Starlight Industries. This way we'll put a serious dent in SDC's source of income."

"What if Jeremy isn't convinced?"

"If he gives you a hard time, tell him your bank has come up with some questionable dealings on the part of SDC. No matter what, you are not to tell Jeremy the real reason. This is very important, Blair. When you talk to your partner, make up something, anything, practical or impractical, and *sell* him on switching companies."

I held my comment.

Dalton misinterpreted my hesitation. "Don't forget the 50K we're giving you for your trouble."

"I didn't forget," I said.

"Good. Your airline ticket will be couriered to you in the morning."

19

The night before my trip to Israel, my intercom at home sounded a little in advance of the dinner hour. I was watching the news on television, dressed in sweatpants and a New York Mets T-shirt. I headed into the hallway, pressed the intercom and asked, "Who is it?"

"Lisa Brandt."

What a nice surprise. I buzzed her in.

She strolled out of the elevator wearing a tight-fitting cream-colored sweater and low-rise jeans. I held the door open for her. She approached and handed me a bottle of vintage Barolo.

"What's this for?"

"I felt bad about leaving the other day without saying goodbye. But I had an early appointment."

"Okay. This makes up for it." I invited her into the den.

"I'm starved," Lisa said. "Have you eaten yet."

"Nope. Do you want to go out? Or should I order something and have it delivered?"

"All-dressed pizza?"

"Pizza it is. Want something to drink while we wait?"

"Yes, please." She gestured to the bottle. "Why don't we have the wine I brought?"

"Spoil me with the good stuff, eh?"

In the kitchen, I ordered the pizza, opened the wine and filled two glasses, then carried them into the den and put them down on the coffee table. When I turned to Lisa, I was smiling.

"What?"

I shrugged. "Nothing."

"Tell me."

"I'm just glad that you're here."

She touched my glass with her own. "I'm glad I'm here, too."

I grabbed the remote, shut off the television, and started my iPod. Adele's voice filled the room from the compact Bose speaker.

When the pizza arrived, Lisa insisted we eat it out of the box, seated where we were. As we ate, she pushed for more information about my failed marriage. "I mean, whose fault was it?"

"Can't discuss it."

"Why not?"

"Still don't know you well enough."

*

Afterwards, Lisa helped clean up, then leaned in and kissed me. Soft, soft lips—teasing. "Tell me more about yourself."

"I already told you everything you need to know." I kissed her back.

We stood that way, in the kitchen, necking like teens on their first date.

Lisa surprised me when she chirped, "Do you happen to have an extra toothbrush?"

"I bet I can find one."

I allowed Lisa to use the bathroom first. After I washed and brushed, I came out and found her already under the bedcovers.

"I know just what you need," she said the minute I joined her.

I cringed.

"What's wrong?"

I removed my pajama top.

"Jesus," she swore. She touched each black and blue mark, shaking her head in sympathy. "Did I do this to you?"

I nodded.

"Here," she patted the sheet, "turn on your stomach."

In moments, very light fingers began to manipulate my shoulders and the back of my neck, then traveled lower.

"Blair—" she whispered.

"Yeah?"

"You're really ready..."

In one deft move she coaxed me onto my back, slid on top, and helped me enter her. It had been many months since the last time I'd made love, so I knew I wouldn't last, but to my relief Lisa came first; then I let myself go, a moan, or more like a groan, escaping my lips.

*

My alarm went off at six. I jerked awake, then looked over, expecting Lisa to be gone. But there she was, apparently sound asleep. I got out of bed, trying to make as little noise as possible.

In the bathroom, I turned on the shower, waited for the water to get warm and got in. Just as it did, the curtain parted and a naked Lisa joined me.

"Wash my back," she instructed, handing me the soap.

I started to soap her back ... then her front.

She had a slim waist, and a small round scar on her upper thigh I hadn't noticed last night in the darkened bedroom. I wondered what caused it, but she was casting a spell on me and I didn't want to break it.

"This is so nice," Lisa said, taking charge of the soap and lathering up my engorged penis. Then, in one fluid motion, she wrapped a leg around my waist as if she were a contortionist and guided me inside.

We quickly got a rhythm going. However, with each of my thrusts, Lisa's head bounced off the tiled wall. I was certain she'd either crack a few tiles, or they would leave a serious mark on her head.

"Don't stop!" she demanded the moment I eased up.

It was thrust—*ka-boom*, thrust—*ka-boom* ... to the point where I became worried for her.

"Yes!" she was calling out. "Yes, yes, YES!"

Will I have to call an ambulance?

"Please, Blair!"

How will I explain it?

"Oh, y-e-s-s!" she gurgled as she came. And I followed suit shortly thereafter.

"You're not bad ... for a toy man," she teased, easing herself off of me.

"How's your head?" I asked with genuine concern.

"Never felt better," she said casually as you please. "Keep up the good sex, Power Ranger, and I could end up falling for you."

20

The airport in Tel Aviv was small, yet functional. I cleared Customs, stepped into the Arrivals Hall and scanned the crowd, disappointed that Jeremy was nowhere in sight. It was rare for him not to be here to pick me up.

I called his office; it went to voicemail. Fifteen minutes passed so I tried his cell, without success. I finally left a message and walked out of the terminal building.

The late afternoon sun was brilliant. The pilot had said it would be ninety degrees for our arrival. It felt like at least that or more. I removed my suit jacket and flipped it over my arm.

"Taxi?" someone called out to me.

The cabbie was short and thin, with dark hair, wearing sunglasses. Jew or Arab? It was hard to tell in this multi-denominational country.

"Taxi?" he said again, apparently the only English word he knew.

I looked to my left. The man's car, a clunker, was not in the usual cab queue. And the lineup of people waiting for taxis stretched for almost a city block.

"Come, come," the driver said, expanding his vocabulary and pointing toward his car.

I decided this option was better than a half-hour wait, so I handed him my suitcase and let him lead the way.

"David Intercontinental," I said once settled in the backseat of the beat-up Toyota.

The driver turned and gave me a blank stare.

"My hotel," I spoke slowly, carefully enunciating each word. "Hotel … David … Intercontinental?"

The man nodded.

The hotel had a view of the Mediterranean, so when we turned onto Hayarkon Street that ran parallel to the sea, I figured we were headed in the right direction.

I took in the sights, admiring the expanse of white sand and beachfront, the crowded boardwalk, hundreds of people sunbathing.

The screech of the cabbie's cell phone brought me out of my reverie. The driver stuck the phone to his ear and spoke in Arabic. The higher his voice rose, the less attention he paid to the road. Soon he was swerving back and forth across the center line.

Horns honked. I felt like I was holding on for dear life. But ten minutes later, we pulled up to my hotel without incident.

"Four hundred fifty shekels," the driver said.

I gaped at him with amazement. "I beg your pardon?"

The man's smile was gone, as was most of his accent. "You heard correct." He thrust out his hand. "Four fifty. Give, give…"

"Four fifty? For a trip that's never cost more than half that amount?"

His look soured. "Okay. Four hundred, then. You give. Now."

I was tired and out of patience. I counted out three hundred shekels and handed it to the driver. "This is all you get, bud. Take it or leave it."

Our eyes locked. The man's hand went to a leather case concealed beneath his seat.

I tensed, not knowing what to expect.

He pulled out a receipt and handed it to me.

*

The hotel lobby was spacious, brightly lit, and crowded. This was a far cry from what it was like a number of years ago. Then, frequent terrorist attacks badly impacted Israel's multi-billion-dollar tourism industry.

It only took a few minutes to check in to my usual room on the fifteenth floor. I was disappointed not to see the phone blinking. I picked up the receiver and punched in Jeremy's cell. It again went to voicemail. I didn't bother to leave a second message. Instead, I shut off the lights and headed out.

The doorman asked if I wanted a cab; I told him I preferred to walk. Hayarkon Street ran forever, with multiple office buildings and hotels for the most part, some only a few stories tall.

I reached the restaurant—Moira's Italian—a little after seven o'clock. I climbed the short staircase and entered.

The tables were adorned with plastic red and green tablecloths. The centerpiece—a throwback to another era—was a Chianti bottle wrapped in basket weave; a makeshift candle holder. The menu was basic Mediterranean fare with an Italian twist.

The owner was performing the duties of maitre d'. Short and robust, she greeted me with a warm, "*Shalom.*"

I asked for a table for two in case Jeremy showed up. This was his restaurant of choice and he knew to meet me here if we missed each other at the airport, which had only happened once previously.

She led me to a table by the window facing the street. I looked around. There weren't many customers. Before she could get away, I ordered a bottle of Valpolicella.

The wine arrived, but I held off ordering dinner. I'd give Jeremy until 8:00 p.m.

The sound of laughter caught my ear. A group of girls aged five or six were dining with two sets of parents at a table at the far end of the restaurant. Each child, a Coke bottle in hand, was shaking it and aiming the spray at one another, their parents either unconcerned or oblivious to their behavior.

I found it common in this country: Leniency was allowed to children while still under the close watch of their parents.

One of the girls now pointed in my direction and she and the others went into a group huddle. They began to giggle. The prettiest one, blond hair down to her waist, moved toward me.

I couldn't keep the smile off my face

"Tourist?" she wanted to know.

I shrugged.

"You like ... Israel?"

I nodded.

She stood there, obviously showing off for her friends.

I admired her innocence and unconditional trust. I took my cloth napkin in hand, flattened it on the table, then folded it into a reverse triangle. I held both ends, brought one toward the center and crisscrossed the other, then started to fold the napkin toward me until it was curled into an elongated shape. I then turned the pointed ends of the napkin inside out, pulled on one end until it formed a tail, and introduced my pretend mouse.

The girl had been watching in mesmerized silence. When I maneuvered the mouse with my fingers so that it appeared to be moving, she jumped back, squealing with delight.

I continued the demonstration, repeating the tricks my father had taught me, teasing the girl with it, waiting for her to try to touch the mouse before I made it jump out of the way.

This went on for a minute or two.

When the door opened, I expected to see Jeremy. Instead, it was an elderly couple, gray-haired, wearing identification tags from some bus tour they'd been on. The maitre d' seated them a couple of tables away. I spotted a cloth bag beneath the table that a prior diner must have left behind, and neither the maitre d' nor the couple noticed.

At the same time, I was just asking the girl what her name was, when some movement caught my eye through the plate glass window. A car on the street had stopped, parallel to the restaurant, even though parking there was prohibited.

The girl's voice distracted me for a moment. When I looked back, I recognized the driver getting out of the car ... and my heart leapt in my throat. It was the same man who'd driven me to my hotel from the airport; and the look on his face told me he was up to no good. He held a device in his hand that he was pointing at the restaurant.

Call it a sixth sense. I don't know why, but something made me dive, folding my body over the girl, sending us both crashing to the hardwood floor.

What happened next took place in the span of about three seconds. The bag I'd spotted under the table of the elderly couple exploded, disintegrating the man and woman in a spray of red right before my eyes. The sound was so loud it punished my ears. White heat followed, burning in its intensity. Metal—nails and ball-bearings like-ly—zinged in all directions. There were screams; horrible screams.

A piece of steel ricocheted off the table's center post and hit the upper part of my back. Another slammed into my head ... and my world turned dark.

21

Yassin changed directions twice before leaving Manhattan to assure himself no one was following. He took the Bronx Expressway to I-95, connected with I-295, then the Cross Island Parkway, and finally Northern Boulevard. Fifty-five minutes later, he pulled up to the address in Great Neck, Long Island.

This part of the operation was vital: find a furnished house to rent, large enough to suit his needs.

On Monday he'd spent most of the afternoon northeast of the city, in Westchester County. A few of the properties he visited would've been suitable if the drive wasn't problematic. Tuesday found him exploring various offers in Montauk, estate homes that fit his purpose, but were not quite to his liking.

He stepped out of his Lincoln and surveyed the area. It was exclusive and quiet.

"Mr. Carson?" The real estate agent, an attractive middle-aged brunette, greeted him by the name he'd assumed for today's purpose. "Right on time," she said, presenting her hand in greeting. "I'm Samantha Saunders."

Yassin knew he was almost a half-hour late, but he let the comment pass. He gave her hand a cursory shake.

"How was the drive?"

He shrugged. "Very pleasant."

"Really? No traffic?"

"There's always traffic, as I'm sure you know. But it was lighter than usual today, for some reason."

"Good, good," she said. "Should we get started?"

Yassin followed her into the house and came face to face with a monstrous chandelier hanging in the foyer. Much of the furniture ran from gaudy to bizarre. Black and white, modern pattern on the dining room chairs, bearskin upholstery on the oversized couch in the den. A huge brass sculpture of a female nude. Walls adorned with garish abstract art.

After leading the way past the immense kitchen, the woman paused and placed her hand on Yassin's shoulder. "Butler's Pantry," she said as if she were proud. "Every house should have one."

Yassin didn't know what she was talking about. He took in the alcove between the kitchen and dining room, replete with minibar and storage cabinets, concluded it was a waste of both money and space. But he noticed the agent wasn't anxious to remove her hand, and her flirtation amused him.

The tour continued, from library to game room to basement; over twelve thousand square feet of living space, not counting the garage.

When they arrived at the master bedroom, the woman said, "Handcrafted bed, bigger than king-size, best if you have more than sleep on your mind."

He smiled at her not-so-subtle hint, which she returned, one eyebrow ever-so-slightly elevated. "And the price?" he asked, double entendre intended.

She guided him back to the kitchen, where she picked up one of the sales brochures and handed it to him. "$12,000 a month, fully furnished. You like?"

Yassin wasn't sure if she meant the house or her. "Yes …
there's a certain appeal," he said with his own nuance. "But I have
one more property I'm scheduled to look at."

She placed her business card in his hand, allowed her fingers to linger on his. "Call me," she said in a way that had nothing to
do with the house.

His slight nod was purposely ambiguous. He headed for the
front door, sensing her tracing his every step. He opened the door
and turned, immediately catching the desire in her eyes.

He offered a goodbye wave, then shut the door behind him
and headed for his car with a lilt in his step. He held up her card and
regarded it for a moment. Then Yassin spit on it, tore it in half, and
tossed it in the gutter.

*

On the drive to the last property on his list for today, he
once again confirmed he wasn't being followed. He arrived at a
street in Lower Manhattan, checked the address he'd written on a
scrap piece of paper just to be sure, then drove into the driveway
and shut the motor.

Another car—an Acura—was parked in front of him. A
short man with an aquiline nose and large brown-rimmed glasses
laboriously climbed out and walked toward him with a pronounced
limp. Yassin observed that his left shoe had a four-inch sole.

"Mr. Carson, I presume?"

"That's me."

"Stanley Vineberg." No offer to shake hands. "You're late."

Yassin seethed but held off commentating. Inside the house, on his tour, he was pleased to see that the furnishings were sparse, the colors drab, with little chance of distraction.

More important, there were six bedrooms, which suited his purpose, and the walls were sufficiently solid to deflect noise from reaching anyone outside.

They descended to the basement. The space here was divided into four more individual rooms.

Yassin knew he'd found exactly what he wanted. But he wasn't about to admit it. "How much?" he asked Vineberg once they returned to the main floor.

"As I mentioned on the phone, the owner doesn't want to be bothered with modifications. You take it the way it is. Minimum twelve-month lease. Ten thousand a month."

Yassin knew his budget could easily cover it, but it was the principle more than the asking price. "Seven a month is all I'm willing to pay," he said. "After all, the furnishings are sparse, the paint is rather dull, and spatially it's not precisely what I was looking for ... but it will do." He glowered inwardly at his charade.

"Nine-five?"

"Seven-five."

"Nine. I don't believe the owner will go lower than that."

"Eight is my final offer."

Vineberg rocked on his feet in contemplation. "I'll have to check with the owner and get back to you, Mr. Carson."

"You do that," Yassin said, already headed for the door, "and make it soon."

It was not until he was in his car that he allowed himself a self-satisfied grin. The price was irrelevant. He would accept whatever counter-offer the sales agent came back with. And then he'd be a step closer to exacting his revenge.

22

«Sandra?» I called.

My hearing was gone.

I repeated her name, believing it was she in the restaurant and not a stranger.

I tried to move; it was hopeless. Time became scrambled. Rational thought turned fuzzy. Then a needle pricked my arm...

I tumbled backwards, praying for a safety net, falling through inner space.

*

"Blair?"

I concentrated with everything I had, struggled to undo my glued eyelids, until they finally came apart. Light flooded in and my eyes began to water. I felt the heaviness of the lids but was determined to keep them open.

"Welcome back, buddy."

I turned toward the voice. A Jeremy Samson impersonator was leaning over my bed.

"The restaurant—" I sat up and was overpowered by vertigo.

I was helped back down, closed my eyes and began to drift.

"Blair?"

Is this real or a dream? "Where am I?" I finally asked.

"Beit Cholim Shel Tikva," the man pronounced the name like a native. "One of the best hospitals in Israel."

"Which is where, exactly?"

"Not far from your hotel, in central Tel Aviv."

"H-How did I get here?"

"Don't you remember what happened?"

Sound stilled. I was gone again.

*

My room was brighter.

I tried to move onto my side. A fierce pain in my back took my breath away. I lay still until it subsided. Then I went to scratch my scalp and touched a bandage instead.

My chest began to throb. I clenched my teeth and waited. My back, my head, my chest. *Anything else?*

I did a self-examination: From my neck to each arm, my stomach to each leg, one at a time. All were intact. I thanked God for small mercies.

*

Later the same morning, I opened my eyes and Jeremy was there—the *real* one this time.

"Sorry for not meeting you at the airport," he said. "There was a fire in one of the factories I work with."

Fire? If the factory happened to be SDC, my problem would be solved. "Which factory?" I asked.

"Tel Aviv Electronics."

I had to hide my disappointment.

"It was quite a blaze. Luckily, no one was hurt. The police think it was arson."

"Terrorist related?"

"Could be. Anyway, I was being interviewed by the police and had no way of getting word to you. By the time I got through it was too late to meet you at the airport or your hotel. I came right to the restaurant—arrived just after the bomb exploded."

"Bomb?"

"You mean, you don't remember?"

I shook my head. "Not really."

"Well—you're a hero, my friend."

"Huh?"

"Yeah. Don't look so surprised."

"I didn't do anything." I went through it mentally: Going to the Italian restaurant, ordering a bottle of wine... *My god, the girl!* "How is she?" I asked, holding my breath.

"If you mean the little kid you saved, she's fine."

It was coming back. "And the others?"

Hesitation creased Jeremy's brow. "Six altogether."

"Dead?"

"Yes, I'm afraid so. And eight seriously injured. But most of the kitchen staff, you and the girl, got out okay. I don't know how you had the quickness of mind. You're more athletic than I would've given you credit for."

"Yeah—I'm a real athlete."

"Hey, don't disparage yourself. You still work out at the gym a few times a week, don't you? It paid off."

All those people, I was thinking. *The girl's playmates, her parents and their friends. The elderly couple that had come in last. All hurt or dead.* "What about the owner. That lady—I forget her name..."

"Moira Feldman? She survived as well. She's the one who spoke to the press about you. She saw what you did. Reporters are clamoring for a chance to interview you."

"Did she give them my name?"

"Uh-uh. She didn't know your name."

"Good, keep it that way."

"Why do you say that? Don't you want to be famous?"

"Seriously, Jeremy. I don't want you saying a word."

"Me?"

"Yes, you. If you value our friendship."

23

I was grilled by Israeli officials for hours. They opened an iPad and had me look at photographs of a list of potential suspects. The man wasn't among them.

I insisted on being released from the hospital the following morning. If the truth were known, my headaches hadn't quite subsided to the degree I'd let on. But my purpose for coming to Israel was weighing on my mind and I wanted to get it over with.

Jeremy arrived dressed in an open-necked white sport shirt and matching Bermuda shorts, his bare feet adorned in brown leather sandals. I was taken once more by the man's youthful appearance; his red hair and freckles reminding me of a grownup Dennis the Menace.

I was winded from the simple exertion of putting on my clothes. I took a seat on the edge of the bed and asked my friend why I was targeted.

"I doubt it was meant for you," Jeremy said. "Unless you have enemies I don't know about?" His expression changed. "You sure you want to leave the hospital? That wasn't a love-tap to your head, you know. An inch or two right or left and you'd have been a goner."

"Yeah. Thanks for reminding me. But I feel fine." I paused. "What's the word on the Zapwired knockoff?"

"*Alleged* knockoff. The company who offered it is run by an ex-employee of Hillel Electronics. The schmuck stole their secrets and thought he could get away with it. They're suing his ass. The bloody thing will be off the market before you know it. End of problem."

I wished I could feel relief.

Jeremy was quiet for a moment, then said, "Stand up."

"Huh?"

"Stand up."

When I stood, he placed his hands on my shoulders, guided me into the bathroom, and positioned me in front of the cabinet mirror.

Both my eyes were swollen and bruised. A partially healed cut crisscrossed my cheek. A dab of coagulated blood was noticeable in my hair. I turned to Jeremy. "No big deal," I lied. "I've seen worse."

24

Once in the car, I immediately fell asleep. When Jeremy shook me awake outside his office, it took a moment to get my bearings. This area of Ashod, in the central-eastern portion of Israel, catered to small and mid-size businesses. Despite coming here many times before, everything looked only vaguely familiar.

Jeremy opened my door and I stepped out. The strong sun didn't help my weakened condition. "Just give me a second," I said. I bent over from the waist, attempted to clear the cobwebs, then straightened and slowly moved forward.

A small entranceway led to the showroom, beyond which sat the warehouse. On my right was the stairwell leading to the offices on the upper floor.

We climbed to the top and sat down in Jeremy's cramped quarters. Files were strewn across his desk and piled on the floor. I could feel the sweat drenching my clothes. The air-conditioning didn't have the same functionality as back home. While cooler than the outside temperature, it was still far from comfortable.

"So," Jeremy said, "what's got you so worried you couldn't discuss it over the phone? What made you fly out here a month ahead of the date we'd scheduled?"

I avoided his gaze. "I'm concerned about Zapwired. I've invested every penny to my name. You said the product was proprietary and I believed you. But if this isn't the case, I need to know now. I can't be left dangling, Jeremy. Not if someone's copied the thing and will be bringing it out at a lower price."

"As I told you," Jeremy said with an atypical serious expression. "This knockoff will be shut down."

"When?"

"Do you want me to lie? I don't know exactly when. But Hillel has a patent. It's just a matter of time until this thing goes away. For good."

I started to feel dizzy. I shook my head to clear it, then got down to the main purpose of my trip. "I'm also worried about the company Hillel uses to manufacture Zapwired."

"What about them?"

"SDC has an exclusive."

"That's correct. Hillel Electronics has been working with them for years."

"Maybe so, but that doesn't mean SDC is the best."

A frown crossed Jeremy's brow. "What are you getting at?"

I coughed, hoping to hide my embarrassment at lying to my partner. "I've been told Starlight Industries is far better than SDC."

"SI?" Jeremy practically leapt out of his chair.

I lowered my eyes.

"Do you even know who SI is?"

"Of course."

"How do you know?" Jeremy's voice rose a full octave. "Tell me, please. I'm curious."

"My bank told me about them. Said they were a better company. Apparently, an investigation into SDC turned up questionable business practices—alleged fraud or insider trading involving one of their top executives."

My words didn't ring true, even to me. To change the subject, I asked if I could have some water.

Jeremy stepped up to the small fridge in the corner of his office. He removed a bottle, walked over and handed it to me. Back at his desk, he took a seat and reached for his phone. After one short and one longer call, both in Hebrew, he indicated for me to get up and accompany him.

*

The offices and manufacturing plant for SDC were housed in a 100,000 sq. ft. facility, which was large by Israeli standards. The management team Jeremy introduced me to—from a Mr. Rosen, to a Goldberg, to a Lichtenstein—all seemed professional.

As we toured their premises, I realized one needn't be highly observant to conclude that the company was above average when it came to modern workstations and state-of-the-art machinery.

Jeremy's grin was almost offensive. "Seen enough?"

*

Another drive, shorter this time. Before we entered the building, Jeremy explained that he'd gotten this appointment by telling a white lie. "Starlight Industries is new and has been after me to use their manufacturing services. I mentioned on the phone that I might be ready to listen to their proposal, but I'd have to get my American partner on board. I told them you were in town today and we just wanted a quick tour. So don't say anything different. Okay?"

I nodded.

SI was five times smaller than SDC. As the senior partner showed us around the premises, I could see the equipment was new but half of it was sitting idle. It was obvious they needed us much more than we needed them.

As we were leaving Jeremy whispered that there was no way this company could meet our production demands.

*

When we returned to his office, I played my final card, taking my friend back to the time we met, reminding him of how my first bank changed account managers on me and the guy nearly put me out of business, how it was the current bank that came to the rescue. "It all comes down to relationships," I said. "I owe my bank the benefit of the doubt. They simply don't want me dealing with SDC."

Jeremy's frown hinted of incredulity. "What's gotten into you? SDC is reliable and well respected in the industry. SI is so new, I'm not sure we can trust them. Do you want to risk putting out an inferior product? Ever heard the term 'recall'? That's what we'd be looking at. And a wholesale recall of Zapwired will bankrupt us. With so much at stake, we should err on the side of caution. Switching to SI is out of the question. I'm sorry, *boychick*."

25

My flight back to the States was uneventful. But when I arrived at Kennedy, it was pouring rain and cabs were scarce. It took almost an hour and forty-five minutes to reach Manhattan. I went to bed without bothering to unpack and slept for close to twelve hours. I awoke feeling sluggish.

I took a taxi to my office and my secretary immediately asked about the bruises on my face. I used a stock answer: "You should see the other guy."

There were a few messages on my desk. One was from John Dalton, which I ignored. One was from Lisa inviting me to lunch. Another was from the toy buyer at Arrow that drew my interest. Up to a few weeks ago, our Vice-President of Sales was handling this account. But she'd taken a leave of absence, then chosen to make it permanent, and I decided to be her replacement.

I'd been trying to reach the buyer, Marianne Lattanzi, since the change took place. Her message was the first I returned.

"I can squeeze you in tomorrow," Marianne said.

The last thing I wanted to do—fly to Minneapolis after just returning from Israel. But this was an opportunity I couldn't pass up. "Tomorrow? What time?"

"One o'clock. Sorry for the short notice, but that's all I've got open for the next few weeks or so."

"See you then," I said.

Arrow was the last major retailer to be resolved. Despite a planned PR and advertising budget on Zapwired of $6 million, success was never guaranteed. Buyers gave us orders that were tentative commitments, for quantities that could change in a heartbeat.

"Sorry. We're closing some stores," was the typical excuse. It was a numbers game, and I couldn't afford to lose one of the key retailers' participation.

*

I next reached out to Lisa, who said she'd pick me up for lunch at 1:00; no ifs, ands, or buts.

Her vehicle surprised me. Instead of something compact and hot, she was driving a two-year-old, black Ford F-150, a truck better suited to someone with a high testosterone level.

"Nice bus," I kidded as I settled into the front seat. "But does big have to mean ugly?"

She pretended to be insulted. "Aw—you don't like my baby?"

"No, no. Are you kidding? I *love* it."

She went to kiss me on the cheek; came up short. "My God!" She reached a hand to my face. "What the hell happened to you?"

"Zigged when I should have zagged?"

"Blair!"

"It's nothing. I had a little accident."

"Little? What's going on?"

"I told you."

"Yeah. You had an *accident!*"

*

She picked a place on Third Avenue. We no sooner finished our burgers when Lisa demanded to know where I'd been, and who beat me up.

"I didn't get beaten up," I said. "I had a small problem … in Israel."

"You really like playing the 'man of mystery', don't you?" Lisa took my hand in hers. "I missed you. And to show you how much, I want to treat you to dinner tomorrow night at Il Mulino."

"Tomorrow? I can't. I have to meet the Arrow buyer in Minneapolis. Not sure what time I'll be back."

"How's Friday, then?"

"Hmm. Let me think about it." I smiled. "Okay, you have a date."

"That was fast."

"You did say Il Mulino, didn't you?"

*

John Dalton was waiting for me when I got back to my office, seated in the chair in front of my desk. My secretary whispered an apology as I walked past her.

"How was Tel Aviv?" he asked before I could even close the door.

"Who invited you, Dalton?"

"I invited myself. We paid for your trip, remember? The least we deserve is a concise report."

"Concise report? I'm sure you already know all there is to know."

"How about you start with the bombing?" Dalton gestured to my chair. "And sit down, would you? I don't like you hovering above me. It makes me nervous."

The thought of something making Dalton nervous didn't compute, but I took my seat and said, with faux naivete, "What bombing?"

"Cute. Do I have to remind you that—"

"—you know everything," I finished for him.

"Exactly," he said. Then, as if the bombing had never happened, he asked how it had gone with Jeremy.

"Our meeting was ... how shall I say ... un-noteworthy."

"Stop being coy. Did you get the production switched or not?"

"Jeremy took me on a tour of both factories. SDC was highly professional, way above average. The replacement you're asking for—Starlight Industries—is so new they have no track record we can rely on. Jeremy refused my suggestion outright. And I can't say that I blame him."

"Didn't you try to convince him?"

"Of course, I tried. Even told him my account manager at the bank insisted on a change."

Dalton's look hardened. "You'll have to go back there."

"I beg your pardon?"

"Meet with Jeremy again, be more persuasive this time."

I was incredulous. "There'd be no point to it."

"It's necessary, I'm afraid."

"Necessary?" My temper blew. "Dalton, I don't know what makes you act the way you do, but I have to tell you, you're a real pain in the ass."

He glared at me. "Not very nice, my friend."

Friend? "Look," I said without calming down, "I don't like to be rude, but I need you out of my life, okay? I can't put it in any simpler terms. I want you to stop pestering me. I tried to do what you asked, but my partner won't budge."

Dalton stood, clenched his hands into fists. "You *will* go back to Israel, Blair! And you *will* let me know when your travel arrangements have been made!"

He turned and left the office without waiting for my response.

26

Lisa arrived at my condo on Friday night a little after seven. I held her at arms length, admiring the low-cut, black leather dress she was wearing.

"You like?" she asked, doing a pirouette.

I followed her inside. "I like a lot. Say, do we have time for a drink before heading out?"

"Lots of time. I couldn't get a reservation until nine o'clock."

"Champagne?"

"Don't mind if I do."

I went into the kitchen and removed the bottle from the fridge, popped the cork, filled two flutes to the brim and carried them, along with the bottle, into the den, where Lisa was already making herself comfortable on the couch.

"*Skol*," I said, handing her one of the flutes, then taking a seat beside her.

We clinked glasses and drank.

Lisa asked how my appointment had gone with the buyer at Arrow.

"Waste of time," I told her. "I waited forever but Ms. Lattanzi didn't show up. I was finally advised by her assistant that the appointment would have to be rescheduled. Apparently, management called a last-minute meeting with the buying staff, no exceptions."

"That's not nice. You flew out just to see her, didn't you?"

I shrugged. "Welcome to my world." I topped off our glasses.

We drank in silence for a while. When I went to fill her glass again, she protested, "Trying to get me drunk, mister?"

"That ... and pliable."

"I'm serious. Champagne does funny things to me, especially when I haven't eaten."

"Would you like a snack? Peanuts or chips?"

With glass still in hand, she leaned in and kissed me. "I'd like something else."

I reached out to take the glass from her.

Lisa misunderstood my intention and went to stop my hand's progression. The glass tipped, champagne spilling on my tie.

"It's ruined." I feigned hurt.

"Poor baby. I'll buy you another."

I looked at her, then at my glass; it was still a quarter full. Without hesitating, I flung what was left at her.

Lisa wrestled me to the floor, her legs enveloping my chest and squeezing. "Give up?"

I tried for a finesse move and accidentally brushed her breast instead.

"Pervert!" she hissed. And she reversed positions, slamming on top of me. Soon, I felt this grinding motion. I spoke her name; she ignored me. She began to undo her clothes and motioned for me to do the same.

I couldn't remember making love this way or lasting as long. When we weren't on the floor, we were on the sofa; often partially on both. The one time I paused was when my injured back banged into something solid and I winced.

"What is it?" Lisa asked.

I showed her the scar.

"My God. Is that from Israel, too?"

I nodded.

"I'll be more careful," she promised. And before long we were lost again.

*

When I awoke in the morning, Lisa was sitting up in bed, looking radiant.

"Did we really skip dinner at my favorite restaurant?" I asked.

"Uh-huh." She gave me a peck on the cheek and smiled. "How's your back?"

"Fine and dandy."

"I feel like I dropped ten pounds."

I laughed. "Me, too."

"I like losing weight with you." She exaggerated the blinking of her lashes, which drew attention to her slightly crossed eye.

I asked her about it.

"Born this way," she explained, then leaned her head against my shoulder. "I want you to always be honest with me, Blair. No secrets or lies."

I sensed a hurt there, something in her past. "Always is a really, *really* long time."

"I'm serious."

"Okay—I promise. No secrets or lies between us."

27

Rain was pouring down when I left my condo Monday morning, but I was whistling to myself. Umbrella protected, I headed toward the parking garage where I kept my car, preoccupied with thoughts of the wonderful weekend I'd spent with Lisa.

Instead of going to my office, I was headed to Secaucus, New Jersey, for an appointment with Killgallon Logistics, the company that handled my warehousing and shipping needs.

A little over a year ago, a MyMart order ended up going to Arrow. The product was stickered with the MyMart code and was priced at $2.00 less than its competitor. It didn't take long for the Arrow buyer to catch the price discrepancy. Even though he'd paid the same cost as MyMart, he was holding my company accountable, insisting on a price concession of over $30,000.

To make matters worse, because the promised ship date to MyMart was missed, I incurred a $5,000 fine. To prevent this kind of thing from happening again, I installed a new policy. Any order with a value of $50,000 or more couldn't be processed without me being present. Thus, the one-hour drive this morning.

Larry Killgallon, the owner, was in his mid-fifties, broad-shouldered with brown hair. He greeted me with a warm smile. Larry was a genial individual and I always found him to be completely trustworthy. He and I occasionally socialized together.

"Follow me," he said, and he led the way to the warehouse where I did a physical inspection of each shipment. Next, I verified the bills of lading against the master list I'd brought with me.

"Everything in order?" Larry asked, handing me a pen.

"A-okay." I signed each shipping document in the appropriate area and handed the pen back.

"Time for coffee?"

I checked my watch. "Uh-uh. I've got to get to my office. Maybe next time?"

He smiled. "You always say that."

"Who, me?" I patted him on the shoulder. "One day I'll surprise you."

*

There were no messages waiting for me when I arrived at my office, but when I checked my cell, I noticed one from John Dalton. I'd purposely turned off my phone for my meeting at the distribution center and now regretted turning it back on.

"I'm at the end of my patience," the government agent warned. "I'll expect your flight details to Israel within twenty-four hours. This is not a request. It's an order."

28

I was up early the next morning, about to take a shower, when I received a call from my sister.

"Blair," Cynthia said in a near-panic, "Mom's taken a turn for the worse."

I braced myself. "How bad?"

"Very bad. Her doctor doesn't think she'll last the week."

God no! "I'll come right away," I said.

"Get me your flight number. I'll pick you up at the airport."

"No need. I'll go standby and reserve a car."

"Fine. Let me know when to expect you."

"Okay, I will. See you soon."

*

I threw some clothes into an overnight bag, called a cab, then headed down in the elevator to the lobby of my building. While waiting, I reached the 1-800 number for Avis and booked a car for the airport in Montreal. I thought of finding a hotel as well but hesitated, finally deciding to take a chance and stay at my sister's.

I punched in Lisa's cell.

"I miss you," she said.

I smiled to myself. "I miss you, too."

"How about dinner at my place tonight?"

"I'd like that, but I'm headed for Montreal."

"Business?"

"I wish. No, my mother's not doing well."

"Oh? Sorry to hear that. How long will you be gone?"

"Not sure. I'll call you when I know anything definite."

*

When my sister opened the door to her high-rise apartment, a bachelorette in the Montreal suburb of Notre Dame de Grace, I was taken aback by how much weight she'd gained.

"You bum," Cynthia said, grabbing me in an embrace. "Weeks and weeks without a word."

"I'm sorry, Sis. Business has been really crazy."

She held me at arm's length. "My God, what happened to you, Blair?"

"Huh?"

"You've dropped about a dozen pounds. Tell me your secret."

"Stress," I said.

She laughed. "With the crappy weather just about gone, I'll start jogging again. It's the damn winter that does this to me. Too friggin' cold to do anything but sit home and eat."

We gave each other another, longer hug.

My sister had been divorced for over six years, living off alimony. With people she knew well, she liked to talk, and for once I found it therapeutic. I became lost in such humdrum topics as our cousins and their kids, and everything that'd happened to them in the past six months. Not thumbnail sketches, by any means.

Even with the added weight, my sister was still attractive. Blond hair cut short, 5' 5", with smooth wrinkle-free skin, she was marred only by the Anderson curse—the start of a double chin.

I picked up my bag, she led the way into the living room ... and my heart sank.

Cynthia's condition was known as *Disposophobia*, an obsessive-compulsive disorder that caused her to hoard newspapers and magazines, shoes, clothing and everything in-between. In my sister's case, "hoarding" wasn't sufficiently descriptive. Her apartment was an open style unit, its concept defeated by the columns of accumulated goods piled high: In the kitchen. Along the hallway. In the bathroom and master bedroom.

She discerned my expression. "Don't say it."

"I thought you had it under control..."

"Blair—"

I was already regretting my decision to stay here instead of a hotel. I didn't want to criticize, but it hurt to see that my sister wasn't getting any better.

*

We took my rental car. Cynthia drove too slowly for my liking. Besides, Montreal was an easy city to navigate. Especially in May. If this were mid-summer, road construction on most major routes would be reducing traffic to a crawl.

"I can pick up something for dinner," my sister suggested.

"Not necessary. I already booked Gibby's."

"Really? Always Mr. Generous!"

"It's my pleasure, Sis."

From NDG, I took Côte des Neiges and entered the downtown core ten minutes later. A few turns and we were parked at Maison Montclair.

Cynthia led the way inside. There was a strong antiseptic smell in the air, and nurses and doctors spoke in hushed tones. The walls and ceilings were painted an austere shade of green.

The attractive middle-aged receptionist asked us to wait. Dr. Richer joined us a few minutes later and led the way to his office. He was a tall, slender man in his fifties, and looked his age. The first thing he did once we were seated was apologize.

"It appears your mother's rallied sufficiently for us to take her off the critical list. I'm sorry if I made you rush here for nothing. But it really was touch and go for a while."

His words encouraged me. "Can we see her?"

"Of course. I just wanted to bring you up to date. However, I must advise you, her appearance has changed quite a bit. I don't want you to be surprised."

*

Despite the doctor's warning, the apparition on the bed shocked me. Much of the woman I knew was gone, replaced by a stick figure; skin and bones and not much else.

"Thomas?" she said when she saw me, naming my deceased father.

I moved closer to the bed. "No. It's me, Mother. Your son."

She raised a scarecrow arm, yanked the bottom denture from her mouth and cackled, "I don't have a son." She pointed at Cynthia. "And whose whore are you?"

I felt my mouth go dry. Her words had stunned me; my mother seldom used foul language.

"Mom," my sister said, "Blair's come all the way from New York to see you."

"Who?"

"Blair. Your son."

Mom began to cry, tears streaming down her cheeks.

Cynthia bent over the bed, using a Kleenex to wipe our mother's eyes. As quickly as they had begun, the tears ceased. Then she nodded off.

Cynthia turned to me. "I guess we should let her rest."

"Is she always like this?"

"Usually. Or a variation thereof. Some visits are better than others." She paused. "I'm really sorry, Blair. The doctor made it sound like she was on her last legs. Otherwise, I wouldn't have called you."

"No worries. I wish she knew who we were, though."

"I know. It breaks my heart. And it makes me wonder."

"Wonder what?"

"They say Alzheimer's is hereditary. You ever stop and think you or I could be at risk?"

"No..." I hesitated. I'd been thinking about it but didn't want her to know. "We'll be fine," I said, hoping she wouldn't detect the doubt in my voice.

29

It was too early for dinner so I suggested we take a drive.

"Where to?" Cynthia asked.

"You'll see."

As a young man, I'd often end up with a date at the top of Mt. Royal. The mountain separated the downtown core from the rest of the city. Today, Mt. Royal would be subject to ridicule for its compact size were it not for the impressive view it afforded of the south-eastern extremity of the island, stretching off in the distance across the St. Lawrence River, into Longueuil and beyond.

There were no other cars when we arrived, and I could see why. The signs, written only in French, cautioned of a sinkhole. The road and much of the natural protective barrier of trees and shrubbery had been torn away.

I ignored the warning, pulled in and parked. In front of us, void of vegetation, the drop was long and precipitous; nothing but large boulders trailed all the way down.

My rent-a-car was a Honda Civic. I shut off the motor and set the emergency brake before leaning back. "Okay," I said, hoping to divert ourselves from our mother's condition, "who're you dating these days?"

"Who said I am?"

"I know you."

She smiled. "Francois. A French-Canadian fireman. And he's lovely."

"Oh yeah? Like Marcel?"

She laughed. "Wasn't he a beaut?"

Marcel, an abnormally thin hairdresser, practically bald, had the annoying habit of squinting whenever he spoke to someone, as if sizing them up.

"What did you ever see in him?" I asked.

She shrugged and said, "He was pretty good in bed."

"Cyn!" I said in mock horror.

"What do you do to relax, Blair?"

"Relax? I don't understand the concept."

She reached out and squeezed my hand. "I hate seeing you this way."

"Which way is that?"

"C'mon, Blair, you can't kid a kidder." Her favorite expression.

"Cyn—" I started to say, when something hard slammed into the back of our car.

My sister screamed.

I shot a look to the rearview mirror. All I could see was the front end of a massive truck, a blob of blue, pushing us forward.

I hit the brakes.

Nothing happened.

Then I remembered they were power-assisted. I started the car and tried again. Useless. Even with the handbrake engaged, we were being forced closer to the edge.

Cynthia's eyes widened. "Blair?"

"Hold on!"

I knew we wouldn't survive the drop. I released the hand-brake, shifted into reverse, and floored it. The tires spun crazily on the asphalt, making a screeching sound. The smell of burning rubber permeated the air. The car rocked violently from the pressure. I actually thought it was working, that I'd stopped our forward motion.

But the Honda was no match for the truck. I shoved the gear into park and slammed my foot on the brakes. *Get hold of this*, an inner voice admonished.

"Cyn, I need you to do something for me."

"W-What?" She was going into shock.

"Be calm, Cynthia."

"We're going to die, Blair!"

"Listen to me. We're *not* going to die. I promise." I tried to estimate the time we had left; knew it was close. "Place your hand on the door handle," I instructed.

My sister didn't budge, frozen with fear.

I reached across, slapped her cheek, and yelled, "Cynthia! Pay attention!"

She turned to me, eyes slowly focusing.

"We're going to jump out of the car. It's our only chance."

She nodded her understanding.

"I need you to follow my directions. Take hold of the door handle ..."

She positioned her hand, but it was shaking badly.

"At the count of three, I want you to turn the handle, push the door open, and roll ..."

Gunfire rang out.

"Get down!" I hollered.

My sister dropped.

I bent as low as I could in the seat, waiting for the car's windows to shatter. Instead, I sensed the pressure from behind relenting. I slowly raised up, glanced in my rearview mirror, watched the blue truck flying in reverse. Then the driver whipped around and floored it.

"It's safe, Cyn," I said.

"Are you sure?"

"Trust me."

I opened my door, hurried around to the passenger side. Cynthia came into my arms with such force it knocked us both to the ground.

More gunfire, this time from afar.

I could feel my sister trembling. "We're okay," I said, holding her tight.

From the corner of my eye, I watched the blue truck barreling up the road, pursued by a white SUV of unknown make. I waited until both vehicles were out of sight. "Can you stand?" I asked, turning back to Cynthia.

Her nod wasn't enthusiastic, so I helped her to her feet. The damage to the trunk of the Honda was negligible, but blue paint marks stained the bumper. I guided my sister back into the car, closed her door, came around to the driver's side.

"Aren't you going to call the police?" Cynthia demanded once I was seated.

"And tell them what? There's nothing they can do without

a license plate number. Imagine the cops trying to trace every blue truck in Montreal?"

She regarded me as if I were at fault in this scenario. "My God, Blair! What have you done?"

"Ready for Gibby's?" I asked to dodge her question.

30

"Take me home," my sister demanded. "Please, Blair. I'll make you something to eat if you're still hungry."

I didn't argue. But as I drove, I monitored traffic in the rear-view mirror, fearful that the bad guys in the blue truck had called for backup.

I traveled a circuitous route to my sister's apartment and didn't detect anything even resembling a tail. When we arrived at 6:45, I found the identical parking spot I'd occupied before, which I took to be a good omen. I followed Cynthia out of the car and into her building. We rode the elevator in silence; exited on the seventh floor.

Cynthia opened the door, turned on the lights, then dimmed them. "Scotch?" she asked, heading straight to the liquor cabinet.

With the stacks of garbage filling the apartment, it had the appearance of being half its size. Traditional furniture without anything too extravagant. Shades of burgundy and gray.

My sister opened the cabinet, the one piece of furniture that was clutter-free. "Here—" She handed me a bottle of Chivas. "You pour."

I walked into the kitchen and filled two glasses with ice, then tipped the bottle until the glasses were full. I handed her one and took my first sip. Reality hit us both at the same time.

"I made such an ass of myself." Cynthia blushed.

"No, you didn't."

"I *did!* I panicked. I lost control."

"Perfectly understandable. It's not every day someone tries to push you over a cliff."

She half-smiled. "Thanks ... for trying to make me feel better."

*

It was nearing 8:30 p.m. and we still hadn't moved.

"Hungry yet?" I asked.

My sister shook her head. "Not a bit. You?"

"Uh-uh. Let's just drink."

She wagged a cautionary finger. "Not good for you."

"I know," I said as I took a hearty swallow.

"You'll wake up with a hangover."

"I know that, too."

"But you don't care?"

"I don't." I picked up the bottle. "More?"

"Oh, what the hell." She proffered her glass.

We both laughed, but it was fleeting.

"Blair—tell me what's going on," Cynthia said evenly.

"What do you mean?" I replied, playing dumb.

"C'mon, what have you gotten yourself into?"

"Me?"

"Yes, you." She let out a sigh of exasperation. "You refused to call the police ... the *normal* thing to do when someone tries to kill you. I want the truth."

What is the truth? I asked myself. *Do I even know? With all the crap that's been happening? In Israel, then here in Montreal?*

"Blair?"

I struggled to find the right words without panicking her. "Look," I said, "someone's after me, but I really don't know who it is or why. All I can tell you is that I believe it's tied into this new product I'm about to release called Zapwired."

31

The route between Montreal and New York was a popular one. I was lucky to get a morning flight, and was settled in my office before noon. I hadn't had much sleep and was still hungover from the Scotch I'd drunk last night.

A call came in from Marianne Lattanzi of Arrow and I took it right away. The buyer said she wanted to apologize.

"You do?" I asked.

"It was the *Big Kahuna* who called the emergency meeting, and he's not someone you can refuse."

"He's not? Even when you ask a supplier to fly in from New York?"

"Even then. But I did tell him about our appointment. It sailed over his head." She paused. "I felt pretty bad about this, Blair."

"Marianne—you're restoring my faith in the buying fraternity. Oops, I mean sorority."

"I didn't just call to apologize. Name the time and I'll fit you in."

"Just like that?"

"Yes, sir."

"Now you *are* being magnanimous. How about next week?"

"Sure. What day?"

"Tuesday at eleven work for you?"

"I'll make it work. See you then."

I disconnected, then reflected that in today's business world, Marianne was the exception; buyers didn't apologize, let alone care about canceled appointments.

*

My secretary stepped into my office and handed me a stack of messages. "Listen to your voicemail first," she suggested before walking out.

I punched in and found the reason for her request. Most were from John Dalton, and they went from mild harassment to not-so-veiled threat.

Then my daughter called and really ruined my day.

"It's happening, Daddy," she said, her voice barely audible.

"What's happening?"

"W-We're moving. Frank is taking Mommy and me to California."

"He can't."

Silence.

"He really can't, darling. The court granted me visitation rights so I can spend time with you. Are you sure your mother agreed to this move?"

"I t-think so. I heard her talking to Frank. I don't want to go, Daddy!" She started to weep.

"Sandra—please. Don't cry. I'm sure this is a mistake. You know my friend Andrew Sciascia? The lawyer? He's very good. You let me talk to him. Okay?"

"When?"

"I'll try him right now. But he's usually quite busy, so you have to be patient. I should know something by Monday, the latest."

"Monday? That's too long. What if we move before then?"

"Well—if you hear your mom and Frank discussing it again, you reach out to me. No matter the time of day or night."

"Thanks, Daddy."

"Try not to worry, Sandra."

I felt horrible when her "Yes, Daddy" response lacked any confidence whatsoever.

*

Andrew was in court so I couldn't connect with him until late afternoon. He immediately picked up on the urgency in my voice.

"What's the problem, Blair?"

I related what my daughter had told me.

"Let me look into it. Mandy would need court approval. Do you know if she got it?"

"No. I don't know anything. This could be Sandra's vivid imagination."

"I'll find out. But it's too late now. They're closed for the day. I'll make some phone calls first thing in the morning."

32

Yassin was in the makeshift mosque he'd attended before, in Brooklyn, surrounded by a dozen worshipers. He leaned forward on his haunches, eyes closed.

The advance planning was nearing completion. There'd been a few bumps along the way, but his people knew their roles and were handling them well. The lease on the house he liked in Lower Manhattan was signed and in place. Only one last detail was left.

The chant of familiar prayers reached his ears and the service came to an end. Yassin slowly rose and moved to the back of the room where he made eye contact with Abdul Masri. The other man acknowledged him by nodding.

Minutes later, they met outside, with Masri already in the driver's seat of the Lincoln MKZ.

*

Like ports in other large cities around the world, New York's had a pulse all its own. Numerous warehouses lined their route. It was noon-hour and traffic was heavy.

They pulled into the parking area of a two-story building. The sign out front read, G.H. McSWAIN & SONS, IMPORTERS. EST. 1915.

Yassin knew that the business was no longer owned by the McSwain family. Years ago, it had been sold to Saudi interests through an intermediary and was registered to a numbered company whose head office was located in the Cayman Islands. It was one of thousands of such businesses covertly controlled by the Saudis, while appearing to be a U.S. concern.

Yassin smiled at the thought: Americans remained oblivious to what was transpiring in their very own country.

He was first out of the car. He pretended to stretch but was actually observing his surroundings, confirming there was nothing out of the ordinary. Then he followed his compatriot through the front door of the building.

A jovial, pot-belied man in his late fifties introduced himself as Ammar Kouri and guided them inside.

They headed along a brightly lit corridor, past a series of private offices, and stopped at a large showroom. There was modern glassware and stemware. Vases of various sizes. Serving bowls and plates. Decorative pieces. And statues in brass, gold and silver.

"Something for the least—or the most—discriminating taste," their host said.

They were led into a corner where Kouri touched a hidden switch on a display case and it rotated out of the way, revealing another room, equal in size.

They moved forward and the display case turned back to its original position, closing them in.

Yassin noticed risers on tables, recessed lighting illuminating the unusual wares.

Kouri laughed at his expression. "Nothing can beat our selection or price. Come—let me show you our most recent arrival."

They moved along the wall closest to them and stopped at an odd-looking chair, straight-backed with wide arms.

"This came to us from Germany," Kouri said with pride. "It's made of a copper-aluminum alloy. Easy to transport. And great conductivity." He held up a sliding switch. "This controls the voltage. You can push it as high as you like to cause low, moderate, or severe pain … and even unconsciousness or death."

"But wait, there's more," Kouri said. "Come, come…"

There was a variety of knives and machetes, and a broad assortment of pistols, including Glock, Sig Sauer, and Heckler & Koch, as well as semis converted to full automatics.

Kouri then informed Yassin and Masri that thousands of containers arrived at U.S. ports on a daily basis. Customs officials couldn't possibly manage to inspect each one.

"Besides," Kouri laughed. "I'm a legitimate importer of giftware, am I not?"

Their tour came to an end. "Tell me what it is you'd like," Kouri said. "We can have anything delivered to any address you choose in the continental United States."

Yassin excused himself, indicated to Masri, and they headed off to the side. "This is my list," he said, handing him a sheet of paper with his notes. "Make arrangements to pick everything up so our address is not revealed. Use Yusef, if you have to. Or the other one, Ahmed."

They returned to Kouri and, in order not to lose face, Yassin began to haggle over price. Once the total was agreed upon, they shook hands as if they liked each other, then said their goodbyes.

Yassin was more anxious than ever to get started on the final phase. A matter of a day or two, he figured, before it all fell into place.

Inshallah...

33

By Saturday I was a basket case. I couldn't watch TV, or read a book, or do much of anything else. Andrew's contact, Chuck Mlakar—the only person who had the authority to give him the answer—was out sick. Andrew thought he'd be back at work in a day or two. That was three days ago. Not hearing anything, I tried reaching Andrew for a progress report. Each call went straight to voicemail.

I checked my watch—nearly 9:40 p.m. The thought of spending one more second in my condo was unbearable. I hopped a cab and twenty minutes later was munching on peanuts and nursing a Johnnie Walker at Billie's Bar.

I had my cell in my hand and was about to try Andrew one more time when it rang and I noted my friend's number on the read-out.

"About time," I said.

"Is that music I'm hearing in the background?"

"It is."

"Where are you?"

"Billie's."

"Perfect. I'm at La Grenouille. Sit tight. I'm on the way."

*

By the time Andrew showed up I was tired of running various worst-case scenarios through my head.

"I'll make this short," he said. "I've got to get home. I leave early tomorrow for an African Safari."

"You? The guy who takes no vacations?"

He shrugged. "I've been promising my wife for years. She finally got me to comply. No cell phones and no work whatsoever. She has me convinced it's for my mental and physical wellbeing. This'll be the most time I've ever spent anywhere. Five weeks."

"Huh? And what do all your clients do in the meantime?"

"Joshua Bennett will be filling in."

"Him? The rookie?"

Andrew grinned. "I know the two of you didn't hit it off, but he's getting better."

"Don't you remember? He made a typo on a court document of mine. Ended up costing me three grand."

"He's learning."

"Not fast enough, for my taste."

"Give him another chance. Anyway—guess who I just had dinner with."

"No idea."

"Chuck Mlakar."

"Huh? I thought he was sick?"

"He was. Sick of being overworked. The guy just needed a breather. Look, Chuck owed me a favor and I sweetened the pot by taking him to his favorite restaurant. Afterwards, I got him to talk about your case."

I mentally crossed my fingers. "So, what's the deal? Another one of Mandy's lies? Saying things to drive me crazy?"

"I'm afraid Sandra has every right to be concerned. Mandy petitioned the court to set aside the summary judgment that granted you visiting rights with your daughter."

My pulse spiked. "And—"

"The court agreed."

"Just like that?"

"'Fraid so. Do you know this Frank Roberts guy very well?"

"Mandy's boyfriend? Not at all."

"He's well connected, and so is his lawyer. They brought up the child support payments you missed."

"That only happened once and it was only a week late. Three others disappeared because my ex-wife's lawyer moved and he never advised me of his change of address. Once I found out, I made good on them."

"Well, they used it against you and that was enough for the judge."

"Sonofabitch!" My voice rose. "What are you saying? I have no recourse whatsoever?"

Andrew took a sip of his drink and shrugged. "I *am* saying that, Blair. I'm very sorry. The decision has been made."

*

I decided to walk home to let off some steam. When I approached my building, I looked up by habit and noticed a light on in my fifth-floor condo. I always shut the lights whenever I went out; it was one of the things I was habitual about. My walk turned into an all-out run.

The keys were already in hand. I unlocked the main door to the building and rushed toward the elevator. I hit the button. It felt like it was taking forever, so I hit it again.

Wait and see, I advised myself. *You might've left the light on by mistake.* But I knew it was highly unlikely.

Finally, the elevator arrived. I stepped in, hardly acknowledging a woman and her child, either of whom may have said hello.

I hurried out on my floor. The door to my apartment was standing slightly ajar.

I cautiously approached. "Hello? Excuse me?" I stupidly called out.

No response.

I was hesitant to enter so I waited, listening for any suspicious sound. I took out my phone, punched in 9-1-1 but didn't press SEND. Instead, I opened the door all the way and stepped inside.

I half expected the condo to be turned upside down, but everything was in order. I took my time walking through it, searching for anything amiss. By the time I reached my bedroom, I felt a bit of tension easing ... until something on the bureau caught my eye.

There was a business card sitting on top of a child's jacket that I immediately recognized. I'd purchased it for Sandra on her last birthday.

I snatched up the card. It was John Dalton's and had two words written on the back: "Call me."

34

In the kitchen, I took a seat at the table and clenched my fingers around the house phone. My daughter's jacket was a clear threat. I furiously punched in the number on Dalton's business card. It rang once, went silent for a few seconds, then began ringing again with a different tone.

"Dalton."

"What the fuck is this supposed to mean?"

"Mr. Anderson, you don't have to yell. I'm right outside your building. You know my car. Come down and I'll explain."

"No! Explain now, you—" The line went dead.

I didn't hesitate, just grabbed my house keys and flew out of my apartment. When I exited the building, the Buick SUV I'd ridden in once before was parked under a street lamp half a block away. An attractive brunette in her early twenties was holding the front door open.

I ignored her, angrily got in, grabbed the handle and slammed the door shut without giving her a chance to close it for me. She shrugged and climbed into the back seat.

I turned to Dalton. "What the hell are you trying to pull?"

"Blair—" He indicated the woman. "this is Agent Rena Olsen. Rena, meet Mr. Anderson."

"I don't give a shit who she is. What's going on with my daughter?"

"Blair, you need to relax. Maybe this will help." He nodded.

Agent Olsen leaned forward, holding a syringe in her hand. Before I could react, she jabbed it into my shoulder and pushed the plunger.

Dalton said, "You're going to listen now, Anderson, not argue."

"What d-did you g-give…" I lost my train of thought. My arms and legs felt like they belonged to someone else. A soothing calm came over me, but I remained lucid.

Dalton allowed a tiny smile; one of the few times I'd seen one on him. "Congratulations. You're the first to try our latest experimental drug outside of the lab. Cool, huh? Complete paralysis, and yet you are hyper focused. Its intended use is to subdue violent individuals while keeping them alert for questioning. So now you have no choice but to listen to what I have to say.

"I told you about SDC, that they had a terrorist connection. Recently we received a tip that they were keeping tabs on your daughter, most likely to kidnap her, hold her hostage, and force you to back off helping us.

"We spread our net and came up with a lead. A group of men we've had our eyes on for the past number of weeks. My people began watching them, following them wherever they went. Which turned out to be very fortunate for you.

"You see, Sandra had spent this afternoon at the house of a friend, Jody Harper, and got permission to have dinner there. But she was driven home by her friend's mother earlier than expected. She was about to call out her hello when she heard her mom and Frank talking in their bedroom. She crept up to the door and listened. Mandy was telling Frank that she'd already spoken to your daughter's school, requested a records transfer, and that their move could now proceed as planned."

How does he know all this? I wanted to ask, but I was still frozen.

"Hearing confirmation that the move to California was imminent, Sandra panicked. She called out to her mother that she was home and going to bed. But she had no intention of doing so. She remained awake until she heard the toilet flushing, and soon afterwards Frank or Mandy—possibly both—were snoring.

"It was just past 10:00 p.m. Your daughter apparently remembered what you'd said, that if she heard her mother discussing the move to LA again, she was to connect with you right away.

"Sandra raided her piggybank, pocketed a little over $20, put on her jacket and slipped out of the house. Her intention was to find a taxi or bus—whichever she spotted first—and take it to your place, an address she knew by heart. But she didn't get very far."

I noticed I was holding my breath.

"A dark-gray van pulled up. Two guys in ski masks jumped out and started for your daughter. Luckily, these were the very men my team had been keeping track of. My agents flew out of their own vehicle, drew their weapons and fired warning shots above their heads to make sure they didn't hit Sandra. The men dove back into the van and sped off. We now have your daughter in protective custody."

Protective custody? I needed to get clarification but couldn't formulate the words. All I could visualize was my poor little girl desperately trying to make her way to me, with no clue of the danger she might run into.

Dalton read my mind. "Sandra is fine. And we'll take you to her. She's anxious to see you. She is the one to tell us exactly how the evening played out. But these people are ruthless, Mr. Anderson, and will stop at nothing. It'll be best if she remains with us for the time being. Meanwhile, you need to convince Jeremy to switch manufacturers. To make it more palatable, I'm going to offer a quid pro quo: You go back to Israel and do what I've asked, and I will guarantee that your daughter doesn't leave New York, even if Mandy moves to California."

"H-How—" I started to say, the drug wearing off, albeit slowly, "c-can you k-know t-that?"

"Beg your pardon?"

I repeated the question.

"Easy. Sandra also told us about what your ex-wife has planned. We'll get the judge who heard your original case to recuse himself. Judge Carmichael, who owes us a favor—never mind why—will be appointed. Believe me, Mandy won't be buying your daughter beachwear. Ever. So, do we have a deal?"

My voice had returned. "What if Jeremy still won't cooperate?"

He shrugged. "Make him … now that you understand what's at stake. But not a word about your daughter. I mean it, Blair. Do not take this lightly. We still haven't learned what Jeremy knows, or doesn't know, or whose side he's even on."

35

After I accepted, Dalton told me I'd have to be blindfolded. The address where I was being taken was a top-secret safe house that BIS used in emergencies. Olsen reached over the seat, placed the blindfold over my eyes, and tied it. The drive took close to 45 minutes.

I was helped out of the vehicle by Dalton, up a short flight of stairs, and inside. Then I was led into the room where Sandra was being held. My blindfold was no sooner removed when my daughter came charging into my arms.

Rena Olsen and Dalton were standing beside us. I asked them to please leave and give us some privacy. They appeared reluctant but nevertheless obeyed.

Sandra was her perky self. I didn't know what story they'd fed her, but it had apparently worked. I planted a kiss on the top of her head and told her I loved her.

"I love you, too, Daddy," she said. "And it's all true. I heard them talking. Mom and Frank are moving to California and taking me with them. They don't care if I ever see you again." Her tears welled up.

I gave her shoulders a gentle squeeze. "Listen carefully: It isn't going to happen. You mother and Frank might be moving, but you are not going with them."

"H-How do you know?"

"I—uh—can't tell you that. You have to trust me, darling. You'll be staying in good old New York."

She smiled, gradually at first, until it blossomed. "Really, Daddy?"

"Really."

The room we were in was of average size, with a closet, dresser, and its own bathroom. I led her to the bed and sat down beside her. "I have to take a trip to see 'Uncle' Jeremy," I said, "but I won't be gone very long. While I'm away you'll be staying here. These people work for the government and they'll take good care of you—protect you from those bad guys in that van who wanted to hurt you—until I get back."

I held my breath and waited. Sandra shrugged and said that was fine. But I couldn't tell if she was putting on a brave front for my benefit.

*

Dalton blindfolded me once again. As he led me out of the house, I had an ominous feeling. The gray van story seemed too pat. The whole BIS thing didn't quite add up. Something was being kept from me. There was no way I could put my full trust in John Dalton.

We descended the stairs and he guided me into the back seat of what I assumed was his vehicle, and we were off. After a few miles of right and left turns, obviously meant to make sure I couldn't get my bearings, he reached over and removed the blindfold.

Olsen was in the front passenger seat. I'd never seen the driver before—male, in his mid-thirties. He introduced himself as Agent Ian Atkins.

The night was clear. I could pick out the rebuilt World Trade Center in the near distance, sitting on the same site as the original Twin Towers.

We were approaching FDR Drive when Dalton explained: "You'll have to talk to Mandy tonight. It's almost midnight. Late, but it could be worse. You'll be driven there now. We can't take a chance on her waking up in the morning and finding Sandra missing. Explain to her that this terrorist group that the government has had under suspicion has been tailing you. Your daughter overheard her discussion with Frank about taking her to LA so she left the house to try to find you. Keep this part brief: terrorists targeted her, we intervened, and now she's in temporary protective custody. It's doubtful your ex will believe you, so give her this..."

Dalton handed me a different business card. It had his name, followed by "U.S. Protective Services" and a phone number.

He continued: "When Mandy calls, I'll back up your story, and make sure she understands she is not to tell *anyone*. And especially not to call the police, since we are not working with them at this point. They're not in the loop. If the cops become involved and fight us for jurisdiction, it'll make our job more difficult. And it'll be a lot longer before we're able to release your daughter."

"What about Mandy's boyfriend?" I asked.

"Roberts? Don't worry about Frank. I'll speak to him. When I'm through, he won't be talking to anyone, especially his lawyer."

A horn honked behind us and we pulled over to the curb.

"That's my ride," Dalton said. "Rena will be with you the rest of the way. I'll be returning to the safe house to await Mandy's call. I'll have her talk to Sandra to ease her fears. Any other questions?"

I had plenty, but I shook my head, then watched as Dalton exited the SUV.

*

We pulled up at Mandy's house. Olsen looked over her shoulder. "Keep it short, Mr. Anderson. Agent Atkins and I will be waiting to drive you home."

I stepped out of the vehicle, took my phone in hand, and punched in my ex's number. Mandy always kept her iPhone on her nightstand by the bed, on soft ring, which wouldn't matter because I'd been told Frank was a heavy sleeper.

I was almost at the front door when she answered in a groggy voice. "H-Hello?"

"It's me," I said. "I'm right outside and we need to talk."

"Go away, Blair."

"Go look in Sandra's room, then let me in."

The phone went dead.

Less than a minute later, my ex threw open the door and demanded, "What's going—" She stopped short, clearly expecting to see our daughter standing beside me. "Where's Sandra?" she yelled.

I ushered Mandy back inside and closed the door behind me.

"Blair, if you think—"

"For once in your life, you need to shut up and listen." I gave her the spiel that Dalton coached me on, pretty much word for word.

"Bullshit!" she spat. "You're a goddamn liar!"

I produced Dalton's card. "Call him."

She snatched the card from my hand, went charging into her bedroom and returned seconds later with her phone. She stared at Dalton's card for a moment in obvious disbelief, then entered his number.

I stood in the foyer, listening in on the one-way conversation. Mandy nodded occasionally and repeated "Uh-huh" too many times. Her questions were often interrupted by what I assumed were Dalton's ready answers. Then her voice went from combative to conciliatory. "Thank you very much, sir."

There was a pause. Then: "Darling? Are you okay? Are they treating you alright?"

A minute or so later, Mandy was yelling, "Frank! Frank! Get out here! Now!"

He came out of the bedroom, half asleep, hair badly in need of a comb-over. When I came into focus, he rose to his full height and exclaimed, "What the hell are you doing here, Blair?"

"Just leaving," I replied and pointed to Mandy's phone. "You're up, *numbnuts!*" I turned to let myself out.

36

I was in my office Monday morning, pondering my dilemma. I'd agreed to return to Israel but hadn't a clue how to convince Jeremy of the necessity of my trip. I was weighing various ideas—none of which I liked—when Jeremy reached out to me via Skype, and I figured I'd caught a break.

"We have a problem with our lawsuit," he opened.

The video feed came into focus. My own face popped up in the top left-hand corner of my computer screen. "What problem?"

"We served them papers last week. To my surprise, we got served in return." Jeremy sighed. "Looks like it won't be as quick a process as I thought."

"So what does this mean for our launch?"

"Nothing. It means nothing, *boychick*. That's why I'm talking to you, in case you hear more rumors. Ninth Wave Electronics isn't going to go away quietly. Fine. Our lawyer assures me we'll still end up winning in the end. Meanwhile, carry on like normal. Okay? Remain confident."

"I can't remain confident after what you just told me, Jeremy. Look—it would be best if we discussed this in person. I'll hop on the redeye and see you tomorrow afternoon."

"Tomorrow?"

"Yup." I sensed his hesitation, but my friend had presented me with the perfect opening.

"Hold on…" The screen became scrambled, along with his voice.

I disconnected. He tried making contact again; I ignored him. Ten minutes later, I emailed my flight information.

*

I called my secretary into my office.

"Nora, I have an appointment with Marianne Lattanzi of Arrow for tomorrow at 11:00 a.m. But as you know, I'm off to Israel tonight, so I need you to go in my place. Don't over-explain. Just give Marianne the sample and let her try it for herself. She needs to see how Zapwired works. Then do your best to get her to place an order."

Nora's face lit up. "Really? You finally trust me enough to have a face-to-face with a buyer?"

I was taken aback. "What do you mean? I've always trusted you."

"Yeah. To do the follow-up. Never to take the lead."

"Well, congratulations. You've been promoted."

*

Lisa reached me on my cell and asked how my mother was doing. I explained about the false alarm.

"Well, that's good news," she said with relief. "Let's celebrate. I can come over tonight."

"I can't, I'm sorry."

"Why not?" There was disappointment in her voice.

"I have to go on another trip."

"Where to now?"

"Israel."

"Again?"

"'Fraid so."

"I want her name and number."

"Whose?"

"The girl you've obviously got stashed away in Tel Aviv."

37

Jeremy was at Ben Gurion when I arrived a little after five in the afternoon, dressed in mustard-colored shorts and beige-flowered short-sleeved shirt. As usual, what he was wearing made me feel conspicuous in my suit and tie.

"You okay?" he asked once we were on the road.

He was driving a new Audi A8, so I asked him how he liked it.

"It handles better than any other car I've owned. But enough about me. You ready to get down to business now, or should we wait until we get to your hotel?"

"Hotel," I said.

"Fine. But relax, would you? You've either had too much coffee, or your nerves are getting jumpy all on their own."

*

I checked in, went to my room and tossed my carry-on onto the bed, then went downstairs to the bar where Jeremy was waiting.

"So, tell me," he said, "why the need to talk face-to-face?"

"You know the reason."

"If you mean the lawsuit, I don't believe you."

"What's not to believe? You promised the knockoff would be crushed. Now Ninth Wave is countersuing."

"They can countersue all they like. In the end, we'll win. And the judge will order them to pull their product and make it disappear. How do I know? I've dealt with this bullshit before. But it doesn't matter. Less than one percent of knockoffs of TV-advertised toys ever make it, right? And that's only if the original meets with success. So, for today, it's not an issue. But I know the real reason you've come all the way here. You want me to switch manufacturers. And you should know, I'm not about to change my mind, even if you come back six more times."

Jeremy had ordered my usual Scotch for me. I picked up my glass and took a few sips. "It won't hurt to do this, Jeremy."

"So, I was right about the reason for your visit?"

I could see the disappointment in his eyes.

*

Jeremy drained his Coke. "How many years have I known you?"

I shrugged. "Seven? Eight?"

"Nine years this October. In all that time, all you and I ever talk about is business. Little else. Oh—sorry—and girls. That, too."

"On your part, maybe. Not mine."

"It doesn't matter whose part. I talk, you listen."

"So?"

"It's time to broaden your horizons, get a little more personal. For some reason, you're fixated on an agenda and I'm bound and determined to find out why that is. I can tell when something's bothering you. You haven't been yourself for a while."

I didn't comment, and Jeremy let it go. For now. But sure as I was sitting there, he'd bring it up again later.

I finished my drink and we headed to the main dining room, where the buffet spread was extensive, from a variety of fresh fish, to hummus, couscous, as well as roast beef a chef was carving.

I was too nervous to eat anything substantial and ended up choosing a small green salad. Jeremy, on the other hand, heaped more onto his plate than the plate seemed able to hold.

"I see you're not very hungry, either," I joked.

He let out a surprised laugh. "That's the spirit, Blair. Lighten up. And go get some real food, will ya?"

"You eat, I'll talk," I said, getting dead serious again. "I need you to make the switch to SI."

"You do?"

"What's the grin for?"

"Because you have this bug up your ass that I still can't figure out."

"I'm just asking you, as my friend, for a favor."

"I still don't get why it's so important to you."

"I explained it all on my last trip. My bank—"

"Fuck your bank!" He slammed his fist on the table, narrowly missing his plate.

I caught the curious looks from people dining next to us.

"Your bank can't tell you how to run your business!" he continued. "I happen to know there's more than one bank in New York. So, screw them if they don't like it!"

My spirits sank. "I have to make this happen. Okay? There's something at stake I can't talk about or explain. It's personal. *Please, Jeremy!* We're friends. Your faith in me will have to carry the day."

38

I decided to make it an early night, hoping Jeremy would feel differently in the morning. We arranged to meet for breakfast at eight and said goodnight.

Once in my room it dawned on me that Jeremy was right. After nine years of being in business together, I knew only bits and pieces of his personal life. The parts I did know were that he was an only child, born in Los Angeles to parents who emigrated from Israel. His father died right after he turned ten. His mother, a breast cancer survivor, worked long hours as a bookkeeper so Jeremy could get a college education.

After graduation, he found work as a salesman in the toy industry and soon became a Price-Co specialist, concentrating on that one account, learning everything there was to know about their business. Eventually Price-Co became one of the few major retailers still headquartered on the West Coast, so his decision had been fortuitous.

Commission checks multiplied. He insisted on purchasing a cruise for his mother to the Middle East, including a stop in Israel. Her ship departed from Athens. She called after she set sail and promised to send a text or email from each port of call.

And she did ... for the first week. Then she went silent.

Jeremy received a phone call from the cruise line notifying him that his mother had taken ill. She was examined by the ship's doctor and transported to hospital the minute they reached Tel Aviv.

The news couldn't have been worse. His mother's cancer had come back with a vengeance and had metastasized to her lungs.

Jeremy dropped everything and flew to Israel. His mother had sacrificed so much for him, he refused to allow her to fight this battle on her own.

She told him about her secret desire to remain in the country of her birth, to be buried there. Jeremy returned to California and transitioned his sales agency to a friend. When he came back to Israel, he opened a toy distributorship, representing many of the lines he was selling to Price-Co back in the States.

Six months later, his mother passed. But returning to America no longer appealed to him. Jeremy found that living in Israel was unlike anything he'd experienced before. Most people he met had a strength, a determined approach to life, to which he was overwhelmingly attracted.

Yet there was something else, an important point Jeremy had made to me a while ago that stood out. But why couldn't I remember what it was?

39

A Continental breakfast was waiting for me when I joined Jeremy in the coffee shop in the morning.

My friend looked at me as if reading my mind. "Do you recall me mentioning my Israeli military service?" he asked.

And it all came back to me—the discussion that had eluded me. How his army experience had afforded him a unique opportunity. I'd intended to ask him to remind me about it. Now, I didn't have to.

"Well, I'm still active," Jeremy said. "Not in the army, per se. Rather, it's a secret branch. And I'm in a position to help you. If you want my help, that is."

What? I recoiled inwardly, but kept a straight face. *First Dalton, now Jeremy, in a secret branch of their governments? This is getting ridiculous.*

The waitress, as if on cue, came over to refresh our coffees. After she left, there was an awkward moment of silence between us. Jeremy's revelation lingered. I didn't know what he'd meant by it, so I asked him to explain further.

"Uh-uh," he said. "If you want details, you'll have to commit. I want you to tell me what's going on with you."

I excused myself and said I had to use the bathroom.

Dalton had been very specific. The situation with my daughter was not to be revealed. Though now, after hearing Jeremy's disclosure, I didn't know what to think, or who to put my trust in.

At the sink, I splashed cold water on my face, dried off with a paper towel, then stood in front of the mirror.

Last night Jeremy said that in all the years we knew each other, we mostly talked business, rarely about his personal life. And he was right. But what if he'd orchestrated it that way? While Jeremy was forthcoming with certain parts of his background, with others he talked in generalities. In some cases, when I tried to delve further, I now realized, he'd cleverly changed the subject.

So, what *was* the real deal with him? Was it possible he really didn't have a clue that SDC has terrorist ties, as Dalton said? Or what if there were no terrorist ties, and there was a totally different reason BIS wanted me to get the production switched to SI?

I paused, staring at the mirror as if it could give me the answer.

What if, I continued to reason, same as Dalton was manipulating me to achieve his ends, whatever they truly were, terrorists were putting pressure on Jeremy to achieve *their* ends, which undoubtedly were no good?

Where does this leave me? Fact: I can't trust Dalton *or* Jeremy until I have more information. And in the meantime, I have to walk a fine line with both of them. If I agree to accept Jeremy's help in this matter, will it ultimately be in the service of terrorists? I'd be bound to secrecy with him, same as I am with Dalton.

What should a person in my position do?

Ah-ha! Screw both their agendas. I'll stick to MY agenda. Because who do I know for sure I can trust right now? I can only trust ME.

*

When I returned to the table, Jeremy said, "You're keeping a secret from me, and I don't like it."

I felt my pulse quicken. "Huh?"

"Mr. Innocent."

"I'm not trying to be."

"No, of course, you're not."

"Jeremy—"

He stood. "C'mon, let's go."

"Where?"

"To my office. I have a couple of new products I want to show you. And then I'll make sure you catch your flight."

*

I checked out of my room and joined him in the lobby. We worked for the balance of the afternoon, until it was time to leave for the airport. The product presentation went over my head and had been a waste of time. But I couldn't tell him that. Now, I was reluctant to get into his car, and he recognized the reason why.

"We'll talk on the drive," he promised.

Traffic was heavy; stop-and-go, for the most part. Jeremy asked what sales were like with Zapwired. "Got Arrow locked up yet?" he wanted to know.

"Working on it."

"How much longer?"

"I don't know—as long as it takes." I paused. "Look, Jeremy, this is a very nice try, but I won't be diverted."

"Oh, you won't, huh?" He chuckled.

"It's not funny."

"Yeah. I can see that. Well, hold on. Okay? Wait until we get to the airport and I can concentrate a little better."

*

We pulled up to the terminal building. Jeremy parked in the allotted area and shut the motor. He took out his wallet. "Here," he said, handing me a doubled-up piece of paper.

I went to unfold it, but he stopped me. "Put it away. Somewhere safe. It's a contact in New York. I don't know what kind of a mess you've gotten yourself into, but should your situation worsen, and I'm too far away to help, I want you to call the number I've just given you." He put his hand out to shake. "Goodbye, Blair. Have a good flight."

"Wait a minute..."

Time to play my ace in the hole? I asked myself. Our launch was planned for one night in August, with a few of the key retailers in New York agreeing to open their doors at midnight to introduce Zapwired.

I said to Jeremy, "How about this—your main objection was that SI was too small to handle a nationwide rollout. But we both know they wouldn't have a problem with the 100,000 units for the launch we're doing in one State. Correct?" I paused to let that sink in.

Jeremy glanced at me and sighed. I could almost see the wheels spinning in his head. "Hmm," he said, thinking aloud, "Maybe there *is* an upside? I could tell SI I'll try them out, but only if they give me a sweeter deal than SDC. Then, after the launch, I could tell SDC I need a deep-deep discount if they want to handle the worldwide rollout."

I kept quiet, wanting for him to decide.

He looked at his watch. "Time for you to go…"

"Jeremy—"

"Goddamnit!" His voice flared. "There's still something you're not telling me, Blair. But I feel I know you well enough. You must have a perfectly good reason not to confide in me—your friend and partner. So, I'm going to let it go. For now."

"You're killing me with suspense."

He laughed. "Yes."

"No shlt? You'll do it?"

"SI for the launch only. That'll give you time to work things out with your, uh … *bank,*" he said with a wink. "Now, get your ass out of my car."

40

The plane back to New York was only half full. Service was exceptional, though I remained uptight. I'd gotten Jeremy to cooperate, but the battle was far from over. My daughter was still under Dalton's control. I wouldn't be able to relax until she was back with me, safe and sound.

There was a delay in getting my luggage at Kennedy, and I was fit to be tied when I saw the long lineup for a cab.

It was 1:30 in the morning by the time I arrived home, undressed, and changed into pajamas. I picked up the remote and turned on the TV, clicked through a few channels, then turned it off.

I'd spent many restless nights of late; none was as intense as this one. I didn't physically toss and turn when I got into bed, but my head went through frustrating hijinks, weighing all the possible scenarios.

If I told Dalton the production switch was only going to be for the first 100,000 pieces, he might not give my daughter back. But what would he do when he found out, down the road, after Jeremy switched back to SDC?

I kept looking at my watch. Jetlag didn't help. I finally gave up on sleep, showered and shaved, and took a seat on the couch in the den. Once again, I turned on the television, this time leaving it on, watching mindless drivel until 7:30.

I grabbed the house phone, wondered if it was too early to call, when it rang.

UNKNOWN NAME, UNKNOWN NUMBER.

I answered it.

"How was your trip?" John Dalton asked, pleasantly enough.

"Wonderful," I said.

"Were you successful?"

"When can I be reunited with my daughter?"

"Blair, what happened in Israel?"

"I expect Sandra to be dropped off in the next hour. My home or office—take your pick."

He laughed sarcastically. "You're in no position to make demands."

"How do I know I can trust you to deliver Sandra after I tell you?"

Dalton was silent for a few seconds, then said, "Okay. Meet me tomorrow at 11:00 a.m. Take a taxi to Tenth Avenue and Twenty-Seventh. Then walk west to Eleventh Avenue. I'll be waiting on the southeast corner. My team and I will be in the same SUV with your daughter. You give me good news—I'll release her from the vehicle."

41

At my office before Nora arrived, I began checking emails. One of the first I opened was from Lisa, inviting me to dinner as soon as I was back. I called her.

"My sweetie must be home," she said. "Welcome!"

"Wow—hello to you, too."

"Dinner tonight? Your place? I'll cook."

"Uh, I don't know. Can we hold off for a day or two?"

"Can't. I miss you too much."

I wanted to give in, but the pressure over my daughter was really getting to me. "Is twenty-four hours a lot to ask for?"

My secretary walked in, bubbling with obvious good news.

"I can't wait even *one* hour," Lisa was cooing.

I motioned for Nora to have a seat.

"Blair—"

Distracted, I said into the phone, "Okay. Tonight."

"That's my honey-bun," her voice sang. "I'll see you at six."

*

Nora was wearing a tight lime-green dress that somehow made her look even thinner than she actually was. "I did it," she said. "I met with the Arrow buyer, Marianne Lattanzi."

"And?"

"Well, she was disappointed you weren't there."

I tensed up. "What did you say?"

"Nothing. I did exactly as you suggested. I just placed the sample of Zapwired in front of her and waited for her to try it. Marianne is certainly an expert at electronic games, with lots of practice. When she took out a pair of bad guys and got the *joy-zing*, her eyes lit up like Times Square at Christmas. She said it was the best darn toy she'd seen in a long while. She wanted to know the maximum number of units she could have and when."

"And you said?"

"What you told me to say. A total order was required for the year, with a separate quantity for the midnight launch. No exceptions."

"In those words?"

She laughed. "Not exactly. I'm paraphrasing. I know how to talk to buyers. You taught me well."

"Good girl. Were you nervous?"

"Scared to death, if you want to know the truth."

"Well—I'm proud of you. You did a great job, Nora."

*

I left work early, not knowing if the bad *mojo* in my life was over or still in effect. I spent a few minutes setting the dining room table, while considering all that could go wrong tomorrow. Then, I relinquished it all to the back of my mind so as not to raise a red flag when Lisa arrived.

She showed up precisely on time with a bag of groceries. She was wearing a white blouse with a tease of cleavage and a dark-brown miniskirt with a slit up the side so high it hinted at no panties.

"I missed you, Blair," she said, then pulled me in for a soul kiss.

*

While Lisa prepared dinner, I poured a Chianti Classico Riserva.

Her breaded veal was cooked to perfection, with two kinds of pasta—a tortellini in oil and garlic and fettuccini in a tomato sauce—all preceded by a Caesar salad.

I found I was hungry despite what was going on in my life and concentrated on the food.

"A penny for your thoughts," Lisa said.

I took her hand in mine. "I'm just glad that I met you."

"Why, thank you, sir."

*

I asked Lisa if she'd like coffee; she said no. She stood from the table and indicated for me to do the same. I gestured to indicate, *What about the dishes?* She shook her head and led me to the bedroom, where she slowly and methodically removed my shoes and socks, then my shirt, pants, and underwear. She locked eyes with mine and began undressing herself, being deliberate and playful. Her blouse and bra, then her skirt. I was right—no panties; which got me rock hard.

"Come here." I reached for her.

She brushed my hands away, then pushed the bedspread to one side. I made another attempt to take hold of her. She wouldn't allow it; told me to get into bed. I lay down, folded my arms behind my head and closed my eyes. The first thing I felt was the delicate touch of Lisa's fingers, massaging my toes, one by one, followed by the soles of my feet. I shivered with waves of pleasure.

Lisa gently kneaded my flesh—from my ankles to my calves, front and back of my knees. It felt like a thousand butterflies fluttering their wings.

Despite my resolve, images of what I'd face tomorrow popped into my head. Lisa and I joined together, but I climaxed in what felt like mere seconds.

"Sorry," I apologized as we were cooling down, lying in each other's arms. I was tempted to tell her about Sandra's predicament. But I remembered Dalton's admonishment to tell no one. A part of me felt Lisa could be trusted. But what if she did something stupid that she thought was valiant and showed up to help? Nope. Too big a risk. *Mum's the word.*

42

I arrived for the meeting with Dalton fifteen minutes ahead of time. The immediate area was void of security cameras, at least as far as I could tell. It also had to be one of the least trafficked neighborhoods in Manhattan.

Precisely at eleven, the SUV pulled up to the curb about 50 yards away and kept its motor running. Rena Olsen opened the back door and led Sandra out onto the sidewalk. The sight of my daughter sent my heart rate soaring. Sandra waved awkwardly and I wondered why—until I noticed she was handcuffed to Olsen. Of course, I realized, they were taking every precaution that my daughter couldn't break free and run to me. Olsen said something to Sandra and quickly hauled her back into the vehicle.

I was still staring at the SUV when someone tapped me on the shoulder. I jumped. "What the—"

John Dalton had a smirk on his face. "I had to be sure you came alone, so I got here early. What news do you have for me?"

"It's done. I convinced Jeremy to switch production to SI."

"And how do I know you're not just saying that to get your daughter back?"

"You have my word."

"Not good enough."

"Why not?"

"I have to see an actual purchase order from Jeremy to Starlight Industries."

"Christ! Why didn't you tell me this before?"

"Why didn't you ask? Seems obvious to me." He indicated with his hand.

The SUV accelerated, screeched to a halt next to us.

Dalton reached for the front passenger door, hopped in, slammed it shut. "No PO, no Sandra," he said, and the SUV sped off.

*

On the way back to my condo I took a call from my ex-wife. She wanted to know when Sandra would be coming home. I told her Protection Services needed to make sure it was safe to release her. "This'll take one more day," I said. "Two at the most."

"Is there something going on you're not telling me, Blair?"

She knows me too well. "No," I lied. "Everything is fine."

43

The minute I was settled in my apartment I sent a text message to Jeremy, explaining that my bank wanted to see a copy of the purchase order to SI, and asked that he send it to me as soon as possible via email. Then, to add weight to my request, I explained that my account manager insisted on seeing copies of all POs that I placed with manufacturers, in order to support my line of credit.

Next, I called Dalton on his cell and said, "With the time difference between here and Tel Aviv, I won't have anything back until at least seven or eight tonight. I'll let you know when I receive it."

Of course, I didn't mention that after the launch quantity of a hundred thousand pieces was manufactured, Jeremy would switch production back to SDC. I figured by the time Dalton found out the truth, I'd have my daughter back and it'd be too late for him to do anything about it.

"Fine," Dalton replied. "I'll expect your phone call."

*

I worked in my home-office for the balance of the afternoon. Dinner was a tuna sandwich but I only ate half. I had my cell close at hand and once eight o'clock passed I began checking for emails every few minutes.

The PO arrived at a quarter after the hour and I immediately forwarded it to John Dalton, along with my message: NOW YOU HAVE PROOF. WHEN DO I GET SANDRA?

His email back confirmed receipt: I'LL CONTACT YOU IN THE MORNING.

*

I was up at five, dressed in a navy sport shirt and pair of jeans.

By the time nine o'clock came and went I'd run out of patience. I used the house phone in the kitchen and punched in Dalton's cell. It rang for over a minute without him picking up. *What the hell's going on?*

I forced myself to wait until a little after ten when I tried his office. A mechanical voice brought me up short: "The number you have reached is out of service."

I stared at the receiver, figuring I'd entered the wrong digits. I hung up and tried again.

"The number..."

It can't be!

I connected to directory assistance.

"For what city, please?"

"New York," I pronounced carefully. "Blackwell Industrial Solutions."

There was a pause. Then: "I'm sorry, there's no such listing."

My pulse went haywire. *If his company doesn't exist, then what do I do now? How will I get Sandra back?*

I ran through a mental list of who I could call. Andrew Sciascia's name came up. But he was away, on his damn safari. And the last thing I'd do is reach out to Joshua Bennett, his still-wet-behind-the-ears assistant. That pretty much left Jeremy.

A text rather than a phone call would avoid the need for an explanation, so I sent it: NEED HELP HERE IN NEW YORK.

His reply came a few minutes later: CALL THE NUMBER I GAVE YOU.

I disconnected, took out my wallet and found his note, a number to call in case of emergency. I entered it. A mechanical voice answered, male and robotic: "After the tone, please state your name, address, and phone number."

I did as instructed, tempted to hold on to the receiver as long as possible, as if this act alone could bring help that much sooner.

*

Scant minutes later someone rang from the lobby of my building. I was shocked by the quick response. Without hesitation, I pressed the buzzer, then opened the door and waited in the hallway.

Lisa Brandt came out of the elevator and walked toward me without a smile or a hello. I was about to tell her this wasn't a good time, that I wished she'd have called first, when she said, "I got your message."

"What message?" I asked, dumbfounded.

"Your phone message."

"What're you talking about?"

"Blair," Lisa tugged on my arm, guiding me back inside. "Come take a seat for a minute."

44

Abdul Masri was in a Hyundai Genesis, relieved that he was no longer cooped up in the safe house.

Their men had been running surveillance on Mandy Anderson and her boyfriend, Frank Roberts, for a number of weeks. They heard every word the two said to each other, thanks to the listening devices set up throughout their home. They also monitored all their phone conversations.

A few days ago. they had listened in as Blair told Mandy that Sandra would be returned to her within a day or two. Then, this morning, they overheard her talking with Frank.

MANDY: "No follow-up from Blair. I've left two more phone messages. Even tried to text him. He promised I'd have my daughter back by now."

FRANK: "So what do you want to do?"

MANDY: "I don't know. But this has gone on long enough. I want Sandra home."

FRANK: "Then call the police."

MANDY: "Do you think I should? The man I spoke to, John Dalton, said he was with Federal Protection Services."

FRANK: "Try calling him, then."

MANDY: "I did. No answer."

FRANK: "Leave a final message for Blair. Give him twenty-four hours. Tell him if you don't have Sandra back by then, you'll be calling the cops."

*

Yassin had paused the recording and turned to Masri. "They've left us no choice. A call to the police will eventually bring in the FBI for a kidnapping case. We need to put the backup plan into action."

"When?"

"Tonight."

They spent the better part of an hour, going over the details, leaving nothing to chance.

*

It was now 2:15 in the morning.

Masri had three of their best men with him. He'd picked the strongest and most ruthless. He raised the volume on the portable monitor. Not a sound was coming from the Anderson residence. They turned the corner of the street and parked in front of the house. Luckily, this was a rather old subdivision. The lots were generous; the homes far enough apart for sufficient privacy.

Omar Aziz was the tallest of the group—just over 6'3". A man in his late twenties, he had a shaved head, mustache, and a muscular frame that rounded out at 240 pounds. He was assigned to Frank.

Yousef Fayed was 5'11" and weighed far less. But what he lacked in heaviness he more than made up for in brute strength. Mandy was his responsibility.

The third man, Ibrahim Abdallah, was the driver. He'd remain in the car and act as the lookout. He was wearing the same mic and receiver as the others so he could communicate with them at all times. He was dressed in a white dress shirt and navy suit. He was picked because of his lighter skin tone.

If an insomniac was out walking his dog, or a neighbor came home from a late night out, Abdallah would warn the men, then pretend to be sleeping off a drinking binge. Should the police stop by, they'd take him at his word that he was doing the right thing and not driving home drunk.

Masri grabbed a large carry-on bag and led the way out of the vehicle. Weeks ago, when they began keeping tabs on Mandy and her boyfriend, they'd made a duplicate key to their house. Masri used it now and quietly opened the door. He knew the code and quickly disarmed the entry alarm. He left the carry-on bag in the kitchen and the three men headed for the master bedroom.

Masri put his ear to the door. Once satisfied, he opened the door to reveal Frank and Mandy sleeping peacefully. He indicated with a nod for the men to proceed.

Aziz and Fayed simultaneously snatched the pillows from beneath Mandy's and Frank's head, used their superior strength to suppress resistance, then began to smother them. At first, both were flopping like fish out of water, but within seconds they were subdued. And in a little over two minutes, both were dead.

Aziz began posing Frank's body. A push here, a pull there, and he soon had Roberts sitting upright, as if he were relaxing in bed and watching television. Aziz had brought cigarettes and lighter along just in case, but they weren't necessary. He removed a cigarette from Frank's package sitting on the nightstand and placed it between the man's lips. Then he took Frank's gold lighter and put it in his right hand.

Masri watched with satisfaction. The murders meant nothing to him. Two more infidels meeting a just fate. Good riddance.

He activated his communication device and the lookout
gave him the "all clear." He flashed the okay to Aziz and Fayed and
the men stepped outside. Fayed slipped into the car and positioned
himself in the back, out of view. Aziz opened the trunk and returned
with a naked girl's body cradled in his arms.

She was the perfect lookalike for Sandra. Similar age, height
and weight. She was a runaway, living on the streets for quite some
time. They'd been watching her. She kept to herself and wouldn't be
missed.

They'd brought her back to the house and locked her in
one of the spare rooms in the basement. Just before they left this
morning, she was suffocated, stripped, and wrapped in a blanket.
She weighed practically nothing. Her body was easily carried out to
the car and placed in the trunk.

Aziz now entered Sandra's bedroom and positioned the girl
in the bed. He stepped up to the bureau, found a pair of pajamas in
the top drawer, and put them on her. He set the girl's head just so on
the pillow, pulled the bedcovers up to her chin, then left the house
and joined Fayed in the back seat of the vehicle.

Meanwhile, Masri was in the kitchen, which was one room
away from the master bedroom. He turned all four burners on the
stove to low, put out three of the four flames, then raised those three
to high, intending for the gas to fill the house as fast as possible. He
set a teapot on the fourth burner. Next, he poured water into a cup
until it was half full. He inserted a teabag and carried it, along with
his carry-on bag, into the master bedroom. He set the cup down on
the nightstand next to Mandy's side of the bed.

Masri had left the door wide open. He removed a gas mask
from his bag and put it on. Then he took out a portable meter and
waited. He knew how long this would take and settled in for the du-

ration. The first half-hour was bad enough; the next fifty-five minutes seemed to go on forever.

Finally, the gas meter hit the red zone. Masri returned to the kitchen and shut off all burners except for the one under the teapot. He came back to the bedroom and unlocked the window. It was oversized and easy for him to climb through. Once out, he lowered the window from the other side until there was only room for his hand to pass through.

It was dark and took a moment for him to feel around in his bag. When he located the mini flamethrower, he reached back in with it. Yassin had researched what Masri was about to do. Death-by-asphyxiation would not show up—if there was even an autopsy on badly burned bodies, which was unlikely.

Masri pulled the trigger. A flame shot across the room and the gas ignited with a huge "*WHOOSH!*"

Masri raced toward the car and hopped in, smiling at the sight of the fire now enveloping the rest of the house.

As Yassin had calculated, a later investigation by the fire marshal would conclude that Mandy had made herself a cup of tea and accidentally turned the burner to low instead of off. Somehow, the flame went out and gas began to fill the home.

Later that night, Frank went to light a cigarette and the house became an inferno. Everyone was fried to a crisp. And the look-alike, because she was wearing Sandra's pj's, would be presumed to be the real Sandra.

Mission accomplished.

45

I remained just inside the doorway, waiting for Lisa's reason for being here.

"You called a number that doesn't exist," she said when she saw I wasn't willing to budge.

I was shocked. "You? You're Jeremy's contact?"

"I'm sorry, Blair. I was under orders not to tell you."

"What about 'No lies between us'—remember?"

"Blair—"

I cut her off. "You're the girl Jeremy wanted to fix me up with, aren't you? When I refused, he changed tactics, found another way for you to keep tabs on me. Our meeting at Billie's wasn't a coincidence, was it? You weren't stood up by whoever the hell that guy was supposed to be—Robert? Richard? You feigned an interest and began acting as if we were, what..." I snapped my fingers. "A couple? Yet all the while you were just babysitting me!"

My voice rose. "Tell me—what does that make you, Lisa? Not only a liar, but a whore?"

She gestured palms down for me to relax. "If you come sit and give me a chance, I'll explain."

"I've heard enough lies." I jabbed a finger at the door. "Get out!"

"I'm not leaving until I have my say." She planted her feet. "Yes, I was asked to get close to you, to get you to like me, get you to confide in me."

"Am I right? Is Jeremy behind this?"

"Yes. He was worried. He told me I'd have to invent a creative way to meet you. The plan was to become friends only. I was supposed to tell you that I wasn't ready to get deeply involved with someone. That I was just looking for a buddy relationship. Someone to have some innocent fun with. When we ended up at your place, I had no intention of falling for you. It was the only time in my professional career—" she hesitated "that I permitted myself to become attracted to one of my assignments."

My jaw dropped. "Is that what I am to you? An *assignment*? How many other times have you seduced men ... in the line of duty?"

She sucked in her breath. "It was ... totally unprofessional of me, I know. But like I said, I fell for you, Blair. And now I want to help."

"So that story of you being a masseuse was all bullshit," I sneered.

Lisa tried to make light of it. "I *am* a masseuse. That's my cover. And I'm damn good at it—as you've experienced."

"So, what's your real job?"

"Does it matter? Jeremy asked me to look out for you. And a good thing, wouldn't you say? After Montreal, and you nearly getting killed?"

I couldn't have been more surprised. "That was you, in the white SUV?"

Lisa nodded. "I caught a flight right after you left, after first making arrangements with one of Jeremy's contacts for the vehicle, with a weapon in the glove compartment, to be waiting for me upon my arrival."

"Who was in the blue truck?"

"I don't know. They got away."

"Well, who do you think it was? You must have an idea."

"I'm not authorized to speculate on who it might've been."

"Not 'authorized'?" I reached for the door.

"Take advantage of my offer, Blair. I'll keep it strictly business, if that's what you want, only, please … don't shut me out. Your life is obviously in danger."

I didn't know what to believe. But it occurred to me how I could find out. "Tell me who you and Jeremy work for, so I know who I'm dealing with."

"Sorry. I'm not at liberty to reveal our employer."

I opened the door. "Last chance, Lisa."

"I don't have clearance. It would compromise my mission to reveal—"

"What mission?"

She struggled with a decision, then shook her head helplessly.

I put my hand on Lisa's shoulder and edged her into the hallway.

"Blair—"

"Come back when you have clearance." I slammed the door shut.

46

I headed toward the den, changed my mind and walked into the kitchen, my thoughts in turmoil. Dalton? Jeremy? Lisa? Who's who? Or are they *all* playing me? Each for a different, self-serving reason?

I started to pace the apartment, beside myself with worry, searching for answers. It all seemed hopeless.

My cell rang.

"Hello, Blair," John Dalton said.

I pushed the phone away from my ear, looked at it briefly, and put it back. "John?" I said, disbelieving it was him.

"One and the same."

"What are you trying to pull? You said you'd call me first thing this morning. I've tried everything to find you! You didn't answer your cell! Your office line's been disconnected!"

"Sorry. Office name and number have been changed. We do that every six months—or when an assignment's been completed. It allows us to create different scenarios. But the reason for the delay is that it took more time than I anticipated to verify the authenticity of the PO with the powers that be at Starlight Industries."

"Why didn't you tell me that instead of keeping me in the dark? Do you realize what I've been going through?"

"Look—I apologized! Do you want to be reunited with your daughter or not?"

I clamped my mouth shut.

"This is how it's going to work: Agents Atkins and Olsen will pick you up in front of your apartment building in one hour. You'll get into the back seat of the SUV. Then you'll be blindfolded again. And sorry, Blair, but Rena will also have to cuff your hands behind your back—in case you get the urge to remove the blindfold. Yes, that will be uncomfortable. You can turn sideways in your seat if you need to. But we can't take the chance of you doing anything stupid."

He paused. "Once you're here, we'll reunite you with your daughter, and we'll get you both on your way. No blindfolds this time…" He laughed. "You're welcome. We'll then make sure you both get home safely."

*

At 11:20 I went downstairs and waited on the sidewalk. The familiar Buick pulled up ten minutes later. Right on time.

Rena Olsen stepped out of the front passenger seat. No greeting. She looked right and left. Satisfied no one was paying her any attention, she opened the back door and said, "Get in."

I was expecting the request and did as I was told. Olsen asked me to slide over, then joined me.

She seemed bored. I figured now that I was to be reunited with my daughter, her assignment was over, and she'd be returning to some dull desk job that she probably hated.

Atkins was slouching in his seat, looking even more bored than Olsen, if that were possible.

Olsen pulled handcuffs out of her jacket pocket and held them up.

I willingly turned my back and allowed the cuffs to be applied.

She reached into her other pocket and removed a blindfold.

"Here—I'll make it easy for you," I said, leaning toward her so she could tie it around my eyes.

I sat up straight, felt Olsen reach across my body and attach my seat belt. I shuffled to get more comfortable. Then it hit me. Just a little while longer and I'd be reunited with my daughter. And I couldn't resist. "Sandra, here I come," I said out loud.

But the vehicle wasn't moving.

I waited.

I could hear the driver opening the center console, then I sensed something being passed to Olsen.

Immediately worried, I said, "Hey … what's going—"

I felt what must have been a needle plunging into the side of my neck.

One second … two seconds … blackness.

47

Sandra?

The plight of my daughter jolted me awake.

I was seated in an oversized room. It had two doors, one at either end. My chair looked strange: metal with wide arms, and an electric cord attached to the base. Kevlar straps bound me in place across my wrists and ankles. I was locked in, practically immobile.

For a moment I felt disoriented.

It slowly came back, sitting in the SUV, Olsen injecting me with something.

But why?

*

The wait was intolerable. There was a rectangular conference table positioned close by, with a 40" flat-screen television and a computer.

The color scheme in the room was a universal dull gray. There were no windows, so this was either an interior or basement room.

The door nearest me opened and I held my breath in anticipation.

Rena Olsen approached, her eyes narrowing with what could've been hatred. She gripped my wrist and checked my pulse.

"Enjoying yourself?" I asked, angry with her. And angrier with myself for not realizing Dalton's "reunite" plan should have sounded fishy. Instead, I'd suddenly believed a guy I never trusted from the beginning.

She shone a flashlight in my eyes and examined them for clarity.

"What are you doing?"

She walked out, ignoring me.

Three agonizing minutes later a man wearing a djellaba walked in through the opposite door; an attachment to his white robe—not unlike a hijab that some women wore—partially conceal-ing his head and face.

"Mr. Anderson," he said.

The voice was familiar but I couldn't quite place it. Had I met this man somewhere? When? Under what circumstances?

He removed the head covering.

It couldn't be, but it was: The Arab standing in front of me was John Dalton.

PART TWO
JUNE-JULY

48

Lisa Brandt faced Jeremy Samson in his Tel Aviv office. "I have no excuse," she said, crestfallen, as she reached inside her purse.

Despite the worn jeans and loose-fitting New York Yankees tee-shirt he was wearing, Jeremy still made an imposing figure. He accepted the envelope she handed him without opening it.

"My resignation," she explained.

His cheerful disposition turned serious. "Not your fault. I'm the one who asked you to get close to him."

"Close, yes. But emotionally involved?"

"He's a good guy to be involved with," Jeremy said, trying to ease the tension. "Look—you're both single adults. You told me your feelings were reciprocated."

"Yeah ... I thought that they were."

"What's done is done, Lisa. We can't change anything." He handed the envelope back to her. "Tear this up. I refuse to accept it." He paused. "How was it left with Blair?"

"He doesn't trust me and won't talk to me until I reveal who I'm working for. He more or less told me to get lost. I'm ... not sure I did the right thing."

"You did. I'm the one who should've come clean with him. I tried hinting about it. But if either of us reveals the name of our employer, we're automatically terminated. No second chances."

"So, what happens now?"

"You've got a job to do and I'm counting on you to finish it. Now more than ever. "

"It's the *job* I've screwed up," she muttered.

"Why do you say that?"

"A week ago, Wednesday, I made another attempt to talk to him, at his condo in the evening. He wasn't there. He never returned home and he's not answering his cell. It's like he's disappeared. Gone into hiding or something."

Jeremy stood. "I want you in New York. There's more at play here than what meets the eye. You should be aware—an off-shoot of the Islamic State could be involved."

Lisa felt a tremor go through her body.

49

"Dalton," I said, "what kind of game are you playing?"

"First lesson—you'll address me properly."

"I beg your pardon?"

"My name is Khalid Yassin."

"Fine, Dalton. Whatever you say."

His eyes narrowed. "Do I have to threaten you?"

I shook my head. "You've done enough of that to last a life-time."

"We're not through with you yet, Mr. Anderson. Far from it."

"Who are you?"

He ignored my question. "Let me bring you up to date: I wasn't getting anywhere with you, so I had to become more creative. Involving your daughter did the trick. Our research told us everything we needed to know about you. Your habits, your customs, the way you run your business. We couldn't have found a better candidate."

"I'm flattered."

"What's that?"

"Nothing, Dalton."

His face grew enflamed. "Not Dalton! My name is Mister Yassin!"

I sat there doing a slow boil. I was desperate to know what was happening with my daughter, but was too worried about the answer to broach the subject. Besides, I knew Dalton wouldn't reveal the truth until he was good and ready.

"I guess I don't have to tell you that BIS doesn't exist," he continued.

"No, I get it. Everything was a ruse to get me to switch the Zapwired production to Starlight Industries. But why?"

He gave me one of those *If I told you, I'd have to kill you* looks, then said, "Good news, bad news." Dalton milked the tension that must've been evident on my face.

Finally... "The good news for you is I have no plans for keeping you here much longer. You will return to work and carry on your normal duties. Under our surveillance, of course.

"Bad news... There's been an accident I must make you aware of. A few nights ago, there was a fire at your ex-wife's home." He paused. Then, with mock sympathy, he continued, "I'm afraid she perished, along with her boyfriend."

"What?" *Mandy dead? Can he be serious? Or is he toying with me?*

Dalton tapped on a computer key. The screen lit up with a video of Mandy's house consumed in flames. Firemen were shooting multiple hoses at the blaze, to no avail. "There's more," he said, hitting another key.

The scene of the fire flipped to the background and a male news anchor came into focus. "After a fire in the New York suburb of Fresh Meadows, firemen discovered the bodies of two adults—"

I shook my head in disbelief.

"—and one child..."

Wait! Did I just hear what I thought I heard?

Dalton turned his computer off with a look of self-satisfaction.

Agony ripped through my heart. "H-How can that be?" I hollered at him. "You returned my daughter to Mandy? Then what? Set the house on fire?" I struggled desperately with my restraints, wanting to get my hands around his throat and squeeze the life out of him. "Sandra is dead? W-Why? I did what you asked! Why did you have to kill her?"

He actually smiled as he turned the computer back on.

I could see myself, a thumbnail in the top corner. Then my daughter's face filled the screen.

"Daddy!" she yelled upon seeing me.

Sandra's alive!

Before I could utter a word, the screen shut off again.

"I want you to remember the grief you just felt," Dalton said. "I'll need you to show the same emotion when you attend the funeral ... and pretend it was indeed your daughter who lost her life."

I was appalled; couldn't make sense of it—until I did. "You killed them—didn't you? Who was the girl, if not Sandra? And why, Dalton?"

He slapped my face hard; once, then again. "Yassin, not Dalton! You will show respect!"

I reeled from the blows. "To whom?" I demanded, my temper out of control. "To you? A murdering sonofabitch?"

He calmly reached inside the pocket of his robe and pulled out what resembled a TV remote control.

Yassin turned it on. A string of LED lights, running along one side, all changed to blue.

Both arms of my chair lit up, matching the same color.

He slid the lever forwards. Blue turned to green. I heard a light hum and what felt like an electric current streaked across my arms and lower extremities. It was unpleasant but still tolerable ... until green went to yellow, followed by orange, then to a blinking red. My body convulsed. Each alteration in color had increased the intensity. The pain was fierce. I knew I couldn't last much longer.

*

I was on the verge of passing out when the colors started to reverse themselves, finally returning to blue.

Dalton turned the computer back on for a third time. A closed-circuit picture of my daughter, full-length, filled the screen.

I wanted badly to say something to her, but this time the feed was one-way. I could see her, but she couldn't see or hear me.

Sandra was quietly crying, strapped into a chair exactly like the one I was in, but looking dwarfed by its size. The arms of the chair were glowing blue.

I glanced at my own chair; the lights were off. But Dalton was manipulating the same controller, so it was obviously wireless, enabling him to take charge of either chair at his whim.

A knot formed in my stomach. I turned in Dalton's direction. "*Please*—don't do it."

He stood there with a blank expression.

"She's only a child!"

Rena Olsen stepped into the picture and placed a gag around Sandra's mouth. The view widened and I could see the lights on my daughter's chair switching to green.

I turned back to Dalton. He was sliding the controller up another notch. "Approximately one week from now," he said in a blasé tone of voice, "you'll be driven to your distribution center where you'll okay the shipment of Zapwired to the key retailers' warehouses in the New York area. If you disobey me, if you become incapacitated before the ship date, if you cause any delay whatsoever, your daughter will be made to suffer a slow, painful death. Here—let me show you what I mean...."

Sandra jerked upright.

I couldn't look away from the lights on her chair, now changing from yellow to orange.

My daughter's eyes seemed ready to pop out of her head.

"Please! No!" I hollered.

"I need to hear you say it."

"Yes, I'll do it," I surrendered.

"Yes, who?"

"Yes ... *Mister* Yassin."

50

The church had an overflow crowd; easily more than 200 people. I spotted Andrew Sciascia and Lisa Brandt, along with Mandy's cousins, aunts and uncles. Several of Sandra's teachers and classmates were in attendance. Frank Roberts came from a small family and his father was deceased, but his brother and mother were here to pay their respects. Since both Mandy's parents were no longer alive, her sister, Julia, had made all the arrangements. The woman had been especially close to my daughter. Seeing her suffer tore at my heart, especially with the knowledge that Sandra wasn't the one occupying the third urn.

Julia's husband had been an undercover cop, killed while on duty barely one year after they were married. They'd planned on raising a family. Julia always wanted children of her own so she gave all of her love and attention to Sandra. I recalled when I was still married to Mandy how often Julia used to babysit, seeing the pleasure it brought her, and how my daughter quickly grew fond of her aunt.

I found it difficult to process what had happened. All three deaths had been ruled an accident. Yassin had told me their surveillance revealed that Mandy was going to call the police. Therefore, he had to eliminate her and Frank. The Sandra lookalike was a necessary collateral casualty so friends and relatives wouldn't question where Sandra was.

"We're watching you as well," Yassin had reminded me. "Don't get any clever ideas in your head about rescuing your daughter. The room she's being held in is wired with explosives and the entry is password-protected. The code is electronically changed every day by computer. Only I know what it is. On the off chance you or anyone else discovers this address and tries to rescue her, opening the door without the correct code will trigger an explosion, and blow up your daughter."

The bastard had thought of everything. It was Yassin himself who drove me, blindfolded of course, to my condo. On the way, he informed me that to account for where I was during the days leading up to the fire, I was to say the pressure of work had gotten to me and I needed a short break, so I booked myself into an out-of-the-way motel for a few days. A member of Yassin's team, who bore a passing resemblance to me, arranged for my name and credit card to be used. This motel had no security cameras.

*

The minister began the service. Julia wept; her distress inconsolable. I put my arm around her and she leaned into me. As much as I hated to admit it, Yassin's trick of making me think my daughter was actually dead had worked. It wasn't difficult to recreate that feeling of loss and emptiness for appearance's sake.

When it was her turn to speak, Julia gave my ex-wife and Sandra a tribute that left many in the congregation in tears. I had begged off saying a few words, claiming I was too grief-stricken, and was relieved when the service came to an end.

Andrew approached. "I'm sorry for your loss," he offered. "Whenever you want to talk, let me know."

"I will," I said, then welcomed him back from his vacation. But just like Lisa and my sister-in-law, with Sandra's life at stake, I knew I couldn't confide in him, either.

I'd driven Julia here and now drove her home. We sat in my car in front of her house, and hugged. It pained me no end to withhold that my daughter was still alive. But Yassin had been very clear about what would happen if I talked to anyone.

"I'm sorry to be such a mess," Julia said as she opened the car door. "Please stay in touch, Blair."

"Anything I can do?"

"Yes. Make this nightmare go away. Bring my sister and Sandra back to me."

I watched as she headed along the short pathway. I would like nothing more than to have this "nightmare"—as she called it—come to an end. But I had no doubt it was far from over. Yassin had more in store for me. He wasn't through pulling the puppet strings. Not by a long shot.

51

The call on my cell from Lisa came as soon as I got home. I argued with myself about answering but something made me give in.

"My deepest condolences," she said. "I understand this must be very difficult for you, Blair. I was wondering if you'd like some company."

I appreciated the sentiment and told her so. But I couldn't take a chance on seeing her, on possibly being questioned about where I'd been for the last few days. Besides, all that mattered was getting the living, breathing Sandra back. "Look," I said, "I need more time."

"But, what's wrong with now?"

"I can't do it, Lisa. Sorry. I'll ... call you," I said and disconnected.

I sat in the den cradling the phone. The funeral had affected me. It wasn't Sandra who'd perished, but it just as easily could've been. There were so many people in attendance today, I immediately texted messages to all those I could remember, thanking them for showing up and telling them how much it meant to me.

*

I wasn't hungry, but I opened the fridge and removed a protein drink. I remained standing and sipped through a straw, then waited. No rejection from my stomach, which was as good as it was going to get.

The house phone rang and I checked caller I.D.: JEREMY SAMSON.

"Sorry I couldn't be there with you," he said. "How you holding up?"

"F-Fine."

"That good, huh?"

He didn't know the half of it.

"Is there anything you need?"

YES, I nearly said, but held my tongue.

"Don't shut me out, okay?" he continued. "I can't bring your daughter back, but my thoughts and prayers are with you. Now and always, Blair. I mean that."

"Thanks, Jeremy." I would've liked to have taken him into my confidence, but just couldn't do it. "Where are we with Starlight Industries?" I asked.

"Production is right on schedule," he said. "That's why I couldn't get away. All systems go!"

52

Khalid Yassin was in his car when he observed the tail. Male driver, mid- to late-twenties, in a black Chrysler 300. Yassin wanted to pick up speed but was restricted by the narrow, traffic-clogged streets of Lower Manhattan. A few blocks later he saw his opening and took it, accelerating in front of a taxi, then yanking the wheel to his right, around a corner and quickly pulling to the curb. His pursuer went sailing past. By the time he realized his mistake and hit his brakes, Yassin was on him.

This would most likely be the same faction that was trying to interfere, Yassin believed, prepared to do whatever it took to undermine his efforts. Sunni versus Shiite; Muslim against Muslim. An internecine battle without end, hurting their cause time and again, all for bragging rights; their petty jealousies turning them into rivals instead of comrades in arms.

He thought back to the time the Imam had appointed him to take on this role in North America. Nassar Camir, a man close to his own age, had actually been the one chosen. But during the training process, Camir had allowed his ego to get in the way, twice disobeying instructions, saying he knew better. There was no third chance. The Imam dismissed Camir, and replaced him with Yassin.

As a result, Yassin had learned, Camir treated the rejection as an insult and vowed to get retribution, big time. It was his people who were responsible for the surveillance of Blair Anderson in London, the sabotaged restaurant in Israel, and the incident with the blue truck in Montreal. Each had been meant to seriously disrupt Yassin's plans and make him appear ineffectual. At this point, Camir didn't want to reclaim his rightful place and take over the operation; his intent was solely to see Yassin fail.

Yassin remained close to the car in front. Soon, the Chrysler accelerated, zipped around a truck and a few other cars, then came to a screeching halt. There was an accident up ahead and all lanes were blocked. Yassin could see flashing lights of the police and ambulance vehicles. Typical of New York, there was a cacophony of car horns. Yassin found a parking spot. He shut the motor, grabbed his keys and jumped out. The driver he was following had also pulled to the curb. He caught Yassin in his rearview mirror, opened his door, and ran for it.

Yassin reached for the knife he kept hidden in an ankle holster. His arm went into spasm; his old shrapnel injury that had never healed properly. He tried to fight the pain, but it delayed him. Finally, he managed to take the knife in hand.

The man had hurried across the street. Yassin followed in a zigzag pattern, reached the other side, and spotted him just turning a corner, onto a street with less traffic. Yassin took off at a full sprint, occasionally brushing past pedestrians but not apologizing.

Closer and closer, he got, until he recognized Ali Al-Hassan—Camir's right-hand man.

This kill will put a serious kink in Camir's game, Yassin congratulated himself.

But before he could act, another black Chrysler 300 slammed to a halt, ten feet in front.

The back door flew open.

Al-Hassan literally dove in.

The car accelerated, its momentum causing the door to slam shut.

Yassin stared after it, cursing under his breath. He turned and made his way back to his car. Traffic still hadn't moved. He took pad and pen in hand and jotted down the parked Chrysler's license plate number, though the plates were most likely stolen and he was wasting his time.

53

I was in my office with the door closed. The 100,000 pieces for the Zapwired launch were due to arrive in New Jersey on Wednesday. Thursday I'd be driven to the fulfillment center where I was to approve the shipments to the two retailer warehouses that serviced the New York area.

I was deeply concerned. What was Yassin's true intention? I did the math. Once the initial quantity was shipped, Starlight Industries would earn approximately $20 per unit—somewhere in the vicinity of two million dollars. Was that motive enough? Was this a bizarre and lethal version of GoFundMe?

If Yassin could have three people murdered in cold blood, it seemed unlikely he'd be doing it solely for financial gain. Something else had to be at play, with Zapwired as the means to an end.

I thought back to when the concept of the game was first introduced to me. Avarice had thrust me into this situation, my eagerness to make the big score. Zapwired was to be my ticket to financial freedom. Instead, I was aiding and abetting a madman, someone I could logically assume was going to somehow use the game to further his terrorist agenda.

*

I worked away, if one could call it that. Shuffling paper was more like it. Sales numbers were a complete blank. Forecasting future volume was a waste of time. Over two dozen phone messages were left unanswered.

All that mattered was the upcoming videoconference with my daughter. I'd put it to Yassin directly: If I didn't have proof Sandra was alive and being treated well, why should I do anything he asked? He could continue to threaten me, but I needed to see her with my own eyes.

He said he'd get back to me. And he did, the next day, laying out the ground rules. A direct access-feed was set up through the Dark Internet that was 95% hack-proof, requiring a code to activate. The feed would be accessible only when Yassin deemed it safe. It would last for five minutes and could be terminated at any time of his choosing should he suspect that someone other than me was trying to access the feed; or if anything didn't seem quite right.

The feed had to go through one dedicated computer at my office, in the early evening, when no one else was around. The communication could not be guaranteed every day because Yassin couldn't always be sure the encrypted code was untraceable. It was up to me to tap in. If Sandra didn't show and I received a blank screen or static, it meant I was to try again the next evening at the same time.

I entered the code now and waited. My computer screen remained blank except for an annoying revolving circle, spinning for 30 agonizing seconds or more. Then my daughter appeared. She wasn't able to see me, but could hear my voice. I quickly told her it was me.

"Hi, Daddy," she said, tentatively.

It wasn't a close-up view, and the picture was very low res, so I had no way of knowing if she was under stress or not. "So nice to see you, darling. Are you doing okay?"

"F-Fine... When can you come get me, Daddy?"

"It won't be much longer now," I did my best to assure her.

"Tomorrow?"

"It—uh—can't be tomorrow. But soon..."

"When?" she pleaded. "And will Mommy be with you?"

The picture suddenly pixilated and the sound turned fuzzy. There were a few seconds of static, then my screen went black.

I had no doubt this was a message from Yassin: *Be careful what you say. Don't get cute. Keep the conversations with your daughter mundane. Anything other than that, I'll cut the feed.*

54

The phone rang. Yassin automatically looked at the time: 11:36 a.m., or 6:36 p.m. in Tel Aviv. He'd been expecting the call so he picked up on the first ring.

"Asalaam aleikum."

"Waleikum Asalam."

"What is this 'terrible news' you have for me?" Yassin said to Randy Altman, his man in charge at Starlight Industries.

"I'm sorry if I alarmed you, but I thought you should know. This Jeremy Samson character insists on inspecting our production line. He says it's a standard quality-control procedure. He'll probably want to test a number of samples at random."

"And this disturbs you?" Yassin said evenly. "Why?"

"*In-line*, while the actual assembly is taking place."

"What day did he choose to do this inspection?"

"Tomorrow."

"Morning or afternoon?"

"Morning."

"Even better. Set up an un-doctored run. Let him inspect as many pieces as he desires. As soon he signs off on them and leaves, revert back to the NC-5 blueprint."

"But this will cause a delay," Randy wavered. "As it already is, we are rushing like mad to meet your deadline."

"Make everyone work around the clock to recoup the lost time, including the weekend. Be sure everything is ready to air-ship by next Wednesday, the latest." He paused. "Am I clear?"

"I ... think so."

"You don't sound convincing."

"It'll be close."

"Just get it done," Yassin snapped. "Do I have to remind you of the consequences for you and your family if you don't?"

"No!" Randy said. "That won't be necessary."

"Do I have your word?"

"You do, Khalid. I will not disappoint you."

"I'm sure you won't." Yassin disconnected.

55

When daylight broke on Thursday, I got out of bed with the deep suspicion that the minute I approved the Zapwired shipments, I'd be fulfilling whatever sinister plan Yassin had in mind—something I'd regret doing for the rest of my life.

I showered and shaved, got dressed in my usual suit and tie. Before leaving the bedroom, I took one last look around, wondering if I'd see it again.

The Buick SUV showed up exactly on time, driven once again by Ian Atkins—or whatever his real name was—who instructed me to get into the back.

A thickset, bearded man in his early forties was sitting there. "Abdul Masri," he said in accented English, holding up what looked like a thin electric cord. "Undo your tie and unbutton your shirt, please. I'll need a minute to attach this wire."

We started to drive.

"Mr. Anderson?"

I undid the front of my shirt.

"At your distribution center," Masri said, "you will give the usual instructions to ship the product to the Arrow and MyMart warehouses in New York. You are not to say or do anything to raise suspicion. I'll be listening in."

"And when will I be reunited with Sandra?"

"It's not up to me. But soon. Once the product is in stores, you are of no further use to us. You and your daughter will go home and that will be the end of it." He paused. "Understood?"

I interpreted his words for what they were—pure and utter bullshit. But I nodded as if I believed him.

*

We rode the Westside Highway to the Holland Tunnel and crossed into New Jersey, finally entering the town of Secaucus. A few minutes later, we approached the warehouse I knew well; one of many in the neighborhood—nondescript, two stories tall.

We drove around to the side and pulled to a stop. There were twelve loading bays, seven of which were occupied; truck drivers and their helpers busy with their loading or unloading tasks.

Masri told me they'd wait for me there. I stepped out of the car. It was humid, with rain clouds forming. I began to walk, my legs feeling sluggish. A voice in my head was telling me to disobey their instructions. I may've been wired, but I could always scribble a note, order the warehouse owner, Larry Killgallon, to place the Zapwired product in quarantine.

But what about Sandra?

That damn inner voice again, playing devil's advocate. If I did what I wanted to do, I'd be signing my daughter's death warrant. I still didn't know Yassin's endgame, so why risk it? Wasn't I better off cooperating? Perhaps there was a way to save Sandra, and at the same time figure out what the bastard was up to, then stop him?

The closer I got to the building, the slower I moved. Intuition felt like an anchor weighing me down. I would've given anything to not go in, to avoid making any decision whatsoever.

I came to the main door, opened it, and approached the receptionist.

"Hello, Mr. Anderson," the familiar middle-aged woman greeted me. "I'll get Mr. Killgallon for you."

"Thanks, Jean."

She got on the intercom while I waited.

"Hey, you," Larry said a few minutes later.

I forced my smile, then followed him up the stairs to his office.

"I'm so sorry about your daughter," he said, once he was settled behind his desk.

"Thanks for coming to the funeral." I pulled out the chair across from him and sat down.

He handed me a number of documents which included the inventory list for the 100,000 pieces of Zapwired that had arrived from Israel. Any product that came under Jeremy's purview had to have his stamp of approval. As I started going through them, I told myself it wasn't too late. I could still take Larry into my confidence. All I had to do was put a finger to my lips, show him the wire, then write, "quarantine Zapwired until further notice" on a piece of paper. He'd cooperate with no questions asked.

The indecision I felt lingered, like a dark cloud hovering inside my head. It took away my concentration, forcing me to have to reread a few of the documents.

I still wanted to do something. Whatever Yassin had in mind, I was convinced he couldn't implement it if the Zapwired shipment was frozen. I slowed my reading down until I came upon the last sheet, a sample of the operating instructions packaged with each product. And I did a double take, trying to understand what I was seeing.

One word stood out in the second paragraph, close to the margin on the left side. "Along" was yellow highlighted. And three paragraphs below that, also highlighted but nearer the right, was the word "play." They were not easy to miss.

Jeremy would have assembled all the documents. If those two words were highlighted, he'd done it on purpose. But what does "along ... play" mean?

I was stumped trying to make sense of it. I was just noticing Larry Killgallon growing impatient when I recalled Jeremy once pointing out that Hebrew reads right to left, the opposite of English. I switched the two words around, and "along play" became ... "play along".

I sat up with a start.

For the first time in weeks, I felt a glimmer of hope. Zapwired didn't have to be quarantined. Jeremy was telling me to cooperate, to play along with whoever was running this show, for whatever reason.

And if I'm wrong?

I felt confident I wasn't. And no matter what Yassin did next, I wouldn't attempt to interfere. Jeremy was on the case. Going forward, I'd make sure Yassin believed I was resigned to protecting my daughter, making it my number one priority, and there'd be no funny business whatsoever on my part.

"You okay?" Larry asked.

I figured he must've seen a change come over me. I forced my optimism down and told him I was fine. Then, for the sake of the wire, I said, "Are the bills of lading ready?"

He handed over another stack of documents. "All prepared for your signature."

I examined them quickly, verifying the quantities of Zapwired to be shipped to MyMart and Arrow.

"The 100,000 pieces will go out today," Larry confirmed once I scribbled my John Henry on all necessary lines.

I stood, thanked him for his help, and left. But now I was back to worrying. I remembered that the room where Yassin was holding my daughter was wired with explosives. *I hope to God Jeremy's plan doesn't end up killing her!*

56

Yassin and Masri were seated together in the kitchen of the safe house, having tea. Yassin took a sip from his cup and asked about the upcoming arrangements.

Masri ran down a mental check list. "First, the airline tickets have been secured, paid for in cash, in the names you provided. Second, the group has been organized as you instructed: one team to handle luggage, transportation, and the like. Another to assure that every piece of furniture in this house, as well as utensils, walls, windows and lavatories are wiped clean and sterilized. Third, when it's all over, I'll fly to Paris, then on to Cairo, making my way by land back to Palestine. A few others, especially Omar and Yousef, will take circuitous routes, but follow similar itineraries." He paused. "Is there anything else?"

"No. Good job," Yassin said. "You've covered it all. Thank you. Now tell me how it went at the distribution center."

The other man smiled. "Couldn't have gone smoother. Anderson didn't object to wearing the wire. He met with this Killgallon fellow and I listened in as he approved the Zapwired shipments."

"Did he say anything whatsoever to cause suspicion?"

"Not a word."

"You are certain?"

"Absolutely. If anything, Anderson seemed resigned to his fate. He even asked when he'll be reunited with his daughter. I told him once the product was in stores, he and the girl would be of no further use to us and they'd be allowed to go home."

"You did?" Yassin enthused. "Excellent. And he suspects nothing?"

"Not one thing."

"So—do you have any questions for me?"

Masri shrugged. "Only one—when do we kill them?"

Yassin smiled. "Not yet. We need to wait for the Zapwired launch. Just before we leave for the airport, I plan on slitting the girl's throat. I'd like her father to watch her bleed out. Then I'll do him."

"Excellent," Masri said. "It will be a just ending."

PART THREE
AUGUST

57

I was in my condo Friday morning already dreading what the day would bring. Zapwire's launch was scheduled for midnight tonight and I had no way of stopping it.

The house phone rang, jarring me back to the present.

"Good morning, Blair," Yassin greeted me as if he were my best friend. "I'm having you picked up at 10:15 tonight. That should get you here pretty close to 11:00. This is the last time. Not much longer now and you'll have your daughter back."

"Wonderful," I said, acting like I believed him. *Playing along*, as Jeremy instructed.

I hung up and began to pace the floor, driving myself crazy with anticipation.

How do I get word to Jeremy about Sandra's predicament?

Yassin was watching and listening to everything I did or said. There was no way I could contact my friend in Israel and tell him. I knew in my heart that Yassin had something abominable planned for the Zapwired launch. But what could it be?

I found myself in the middle of the den, wanting to throw something, wanting to scream at the top of my lungs.

My daughter was waiting for me to rescue her. If I could hang in until now, twelve hours more shouldn't matter. What I would give to see into the future and know what Yassin was up to.

I could visualize Sandra in my mind and was anxious to finally tell her how sorry I was for getting her involved. Yassin had allowed our video calls to continue sporadically. In some ways it made things worse. So close, yet so far. Each time we talked my heart bled a little more. Would I really be allowed to hold her again? Even for one last time?

*

As 10:15 p.m. approached, I entered the elevator and rode it down to the lobby level. I was just exiting when an elderly woman carrying a heaping bag of groceries almost collided with me, and a loaf of bread toppled to the floor. I picked it up and put it back in her bag, while she cursed me out in Yiddish. I apologized, then headed out of the building and approached the waiting SUV, idling at the curb.

As usual, "Agent Atkins" sat behind the wheel. Abdul Masri was in the back seat. We pulled away. Instead of a blindfold, Masri held up a cloth bag and slipped it over my head.

58

When we arrived, Masri guided me out of the vehicle, up a few stairs, and toward what I assumed was the entrance to the safe house.

Once the door opened, he gripped my arm and led the way into a room, where he sat me down. As soon I felt the steel connect with my spine, I realized it was the same chair as before. The straps were secured around my arms and legs. I wondered if more torture was in store for me. *Did Yassin somehow get wind of Jeremy's plan?*

A hollow feeling gripped the pit of my stomach. The cloth bag was yanked off my head. Then Masri walked out and I was left alone.

What felt like a half hour passed. For the umpteenth time I tested the tension in the straps holding me in the chair, looking for any give in at least one of them that I could work loose.

About ten minutes later, at what I guessed was near midnight, Yassin walked in, using the door behind me. He was dressed in a gray lightweight suit and matching conservative tie.

Back to John Dalton? I wondered.

"And so your journey is near its end," he said pleasantly enough. "I am sorry if it was not all to your liking. Is there anything you'd like to ask me?"

Play along, I reminded myself. "Yes. Were you serious when you said Sandra will be released?"

He shrugged. "We'll see."

"Let's cut the bullshit, Yassin. You and I both know neither my daughter nor I will be leaving here alive."

He turned his back to me, and started typing on his computer keyboard.

"So," I called out, "how about granting a dying man's last request?"

Yassin ignored me.

"Tell me … what the fuck is this all about?"

He continued typing.

"What kind of bribe do you plan to use Zapwired for?"

That got his attention. Yassin turned around and smiled. "That's what you think? That's the best you can come up with? A bribe? No, no, my friend. I'm much smarter than that."

"So, tell me how smart you are," I challenged him.

I knew he wouldn't be able to resist. Yassin went over to a wall cabinet, opened it and removed a Zapwired prototype with its cover removed. He pointed to an area adjacent to the battery compartment. "You see, your precious little toy has had an internal change. This capacitor is used to divert the electrical charge from what was originally intended. In today's world of miniaturization, the components are infinitely smaller and more versatile. The employees of Starlight Industries, who work for me, only had to insert the capacitor, then convert the starter to a trigger mechanism. Thus, it can ignite this innocuous-looking substance." He pointed inside the works to a minuscule, colorless blob, resembling a swatch of hardened glue. "NC-5—the most versatile form of plastique available on the Black Market today. A fraction of the amount has triple the explosive power of its predecessor, C-4. It's guaranteed to cause a powerful explosion that can annihilate or severely injure a roomful of people.

"Zapwired comes with its own batteries. All the customer has to do is use a Phillips screwdriver to open the battery compartment, pull this isolater tab like so." He demonstrated. "And the contacts are no longer protected. Turn the switch to ON and wait three seconds..." He flipped it. Sparks soon flew, and a sound emitted—"*PHHT*"—like a match flame igniting.

Yassin let out a chuckle. "If the wiring had been in place, you and I would be visiting with Allah this exact moment." He paused. "But here's the best part: the first one hundred thousand pieces have been moved from the key retailer warehouses in the New York area to their individual stores, in time to get their shelves stocked for tonight's launch.

"So, imagine—a hundred thousand homes filled with anxious teenagers, many surrounded by friends or other family members. Best case scenario, seventy-five percent will turn on their units soon after they or their parents bring it home. Then three seconds later, BOOM!" He was thoroughly enjoying himself.

"What do you think, Blair? How many infidels do you think will die tonight? Perhaps not all 100,000. I estimate three-quarters that amount. Can you see the bodies torn apart? The blood flowing everywhere?"

My head dropped. What he described was exactly what I was visualizing. This was worse than my worst nightmare.

"Let me explain what my men are doing now," he went on, speaking so casually, he could've been telling me what he had planned for dinner. "Omar, Yousef and Abdul have positioned themselves in three different suburban retail locations. A customer in each store is being chosen, followed out to his or her car, and then home ... which is when the fun will start.

"You see, we have access to one of the latest marvels of the world. It's a knockoff of something developed by researchers at the University of California, Berkeley. It's described as the smallest flying drone ever made. It travels with zero moving parts, meaning no rotors, wings, or similar appendages. Instead, the insect-scale drone relies on atmospheric ion thrusters, which allow it to move in complete silence.

"But ours is even better, Blair." His smile lit up again, only this time it was nearly euphoric. "We call it Mighty-Bot for a reason. It's not only smaller than a fly, it has the capability to record both audio and video, with little chance of being detected.

"My men will manipulate the drones so each will attach itself to a person walking into their home. Once inside, the drones will hover inconspicuously in one corner. From there it will broadcast the exact moment a Zapwired is turned on and, seconds later, the explosions."

I imagined I was watching that broadcast now, images of blood and gore flashing in front of my eyes.

"Of course, there might be a few hiccups," Yassin continued. "But with all three cameras in operation, I'd say at least one of them will be successful in capturing the gruesome devastation.

"The minute it's over, we will upload the best one—or even all three if they are good video captures—to the major news networks, along with Instagram, YouTube, and other social media sites. Included will be our political statement, making it clear that this is retribution for past American atrocities committed against the Muslim community. Especially the egregious, cowardly cover-up by the US government when one of its missiles killed seven young boys, including my son."

I was chilled to the bone. I could now understand Yassin's motivation. But was that an excuse for such widespread mass murder? I felt anger and guilt at what I'd helped him perpetrate.

The room began to spin. I forced my breathing to slow. Now that I was aware of the full truth, I knew I was right. Both my daughter and I were doomed. No other option.

59

The digital timestamp blinking on the clock in the left-hand corner of the desk showed it was 12:38 a.m. Yassin took a seat at the table a few feet in front of my chair. He positioned three cell phones in front of him. Then he made a show of turning on the computer. "Here we go," he said with overt pride.

The picture split into three segments, each out of focus. Abdul Masri's voice was the first I heard. It came from one of the cell phones, now on speaker mode. He spoke in Arabic and Yassin translated. At the moment, Masri was in his car, stationed across the street from a large house in Manesset on Long Island.

"The drone is in place," Yassin continued, his voice rising in anticipation. "Look—"

The image on the far-left side of the screen came alive with two boys in their mid-teens, a girl slightly younger, and their middle-aged parents standing next to them in the den of their home.

"Masri was able to settle the drone on the back of one of the boy's belts," Yassin translated. "Once inside the house, he maneuvered it until it was far enough away to take in the entire room."

The one piece of furniture to catch my attention was the entertainment center that included a 75" flat screen TV and a Sonos Arc sound bar. What light there was in the room came from an unusual-looking floor lamp, decorated with what could've been Swarovski crystals.

The father had a screwdriver in hand and was obviously following directions for opening the battery compartment. The look of excitement on the teenagers' faces filled me with shame. It was my advertising that had built the demand for Zapwired and gotten them to run out and purchase it.

Yassin addressed the second phone, also on speaker, and once again he went back and forth in Arabic. "This is Yousef Fayed reporting," he said to me, "parked in Queens, outside another house. There is..." His voice dropped an octave and anger creased his brow, "a bit of a problem."

They continued to speak, then Yassin said, "Fayad was unable to sneak the drone into the house. But he will keep trying. Perhaps he'll find a window open. Or maybe a door."

Another view, on the right side of the screen this time, opened up. And a voice from the third cell phone came to life. Yassin listened for a minute or two, and his mood brightened. "Ah ... this one's working. Omar Aziz is in White Plains, positioned outside a bungalow. The Zapwired was purchased by a couple and their daughter in her mid-teens. He attached the drone to the back of the mother's dress."

The image showed a lady in her early-forties, red shoulder-length hair, seated at a table in a large kitchen next to a brown-haired man, who was a few years older and apparently her husband. Their daughter was tearing open the Zapwired box.

I shuddered at what was to come. And I mentally crossed my fingers and prayed to every deity I could think of, asking—*begging*—for a miracle.

To my disappointment, the second phone came back to life. Words were spoken rapidly. Yassin's face lit up. "Problem solved," he said. "The woman in Queens came out to deposit the garbage on the driveway by the curb. Fayad managed to have the drone follow her, and it's now safely inside. Watch this..." He pointed.

The house was fairly modern. The man was tall, overweight, with graying hair. The woman seemed dwarfed by his size. She was a petite brunette and wore glasses. The children, a boy and girl, were in their early teens. They were all in the spacious family room, seated on what looked like a leather couch. A Zapwired was resting on a coffee table in front of them. Each of the four appeared anxious to start playing the game.

I considered the three separate scenes that had unfolded on the computer in front of me. The family of five, the couple and their daughter, and the man and woman with their two kids. All mere minutes away from a horrible tragedy.

Yassin could only just contain himself. "The message will be delivered loud and clear! This will go down..."

He inhaled a deep breath.

I followed his gaze.

The man in the house on Long Island had the battery compartment open, his wife and children gathered around him. The older boy pulled the isolater tab, then shut the lid. His brother and sister leaned in closer. Finally, the boy flipped the game's ON switch.

Yassin was rubbing his hands together as he started the countdown: "Three... two... one..."

The oldest boy began wielding the joy pad like a professional, while his siblings cheered him on. I could hear shoot-em-up noises. Lights were flashing. The boy's forearm reacted with a jolt each time he took a hit from one of the bad guys. And I couldn't believe it. There'd been no explosion.

Yassin's head jerked back in shock. But he quickly recovered. "No problem," he said, "the workers at Starlight Industries were under the gun to meet my shipping deadline. It had to be expected that a few of the units would be faulty. What we're seeing is an anomaly."

He tapped away at the computer.

The feed disappeared and the screen refreshed. The view

was the interior of the White Plains bungalow. The teenaged girl was just shutting the battery compartment.

Yassin bounced up and down. Once, then twice. I could read the tension pouring off him when he said, "Here it comes."

No! a voice screamed in my head.

The girl turned the game on.

Yassin began a countdown again, this time under his breath, "Three...two..." At "one" he was standing on the balls of his feet.

I was watching transfixed when the Zapwired came to life. The girl began playing with a look of exhilaration. Five more seconds went by, and no BOOM!

Yassin cursed in Arabic. "Okay," he said, puffing himself up, "as you Americans say, 'third time's the charm'. This time you will see Allah's will..."

He turned off the second feed and a change came over him. He was no longer calm and in control. His fists were now white-knuckled and his eyes were ablaze.

I peered at the screen. The house in Queens: The boy and girl having an argument over who gets to play the game first.

The boy won and turned the control switch to ON.

I tore my eyes away but I couldn't stop the countdown in my head. *Three...two...one...* But no explosion. No screaming in agony. I looked back. There on the screen, the boy was playing the Zapwired. His family cheering him on. Laughing. Joy. Fun.

Yassin smashed his fist on the table. He went to the computer keyboard and violently punched a series of keys. The screen split into eight squares, each a news feed of various network and cable stations, including ABC, CBS, NBC, FOX, and CNN.

In five out of eight, anchors were reporting the huge success of Zapwired. There were even some instances where reporters and cameramen were broadcasting live from consumers' homes, filming the delighted families. It appeared to take an effort to distract some of the players away from the game long enough to conduct an interview. All were gushing praise.

Yassin turned to me with pure hatred in his eyes. "I don't know how you did it..."

"What?" I said. "I didn't do anything." And then it dawned on me: *Play along.* Jeremy had a hand in this.

"...but you will pay!" He stepped up to the wall cabinet, opened it, and removed a machete. "You are going to watch me grab your daughter by the hair and slowly, with as much pain as I can inflict, cut off her head!"

He went back to the keyboard and tapped a single key. The screen filled with a shot of my daughter, strapped into the damn chair I abhorred.

"Enjoy the show," he said as he departed through his private door.

"No! No! No!" I screamed after him. "I had nothing to do with this!"

60

Yassin was aware of losing control, and he admonished himself. Though it did little good. His fury knew no relief. He entered the corridor in a rage, his heart beating so rapidly he could hear it pounding in his ears. He paused until he was able to think more rationally.

He wanted Blair Anderson to watch the computer screen as he beheaded his daughter. Then he would return and start in on him. Perhaps he'd begin by hacking off each ear, then chopping off his fingers, one at a time. Whatever it took until Blair revealed how he managed to thwart his plan. Have him beg for death.

But...

It dawned on Yassin that Anderson couldn't have acted alone. And whomever he had gotten on board could've followed him to this very house. Or, if they were told the address, they could be on their way. Torturing Anderson might reveal who else was involved, but he didn't have the luxury of time.

Yassin hated to see his mission fail, yet it would be far worse if he allowed himself to be caught.

He considered his options once more. There was no point in dragging this out, he decided. He'd have to do them both quickly. No matter what, he'd return to America one day. He swore this to Allah. And when he came back, he would have something far more diabolical in play.

He was now in front of Sandra's room. Yassin punched in the security code, opened the door, and rushed in.

He stopped short, in utter shock at his second major surprise of the day: the girl's chair was empty, the straps hanging loose.

61

I fought like a man possessed to get free of the restraints holding me, desperate to get to my daughter, never once losing sight of her on the computer screen.

I expected Yassin to burst into the picture at any moment. I knew I'd have to shut my eyes when that happened and pray there was no audio feed.

I thought I heard one of the doors opening. *Or am I imagining it?*

"Blair?"

Did someone call my name?

"Blair! It's me, Lisa."

How can that be? Yet ... there she was, standing in front of the computer screen and blocking my view.

The fear that I was hallucinating disappeared once she began untying my straps, starting with my ankles.

"Sandra!" I yelled.

"Don't worry," Lisa said calmly, "she's okay."

"N-No! Y-You d-don't understand! There's this m-man— Khalid Yassin! He ... has my daughter!" I pointed to the screen with my free hand. "P-Please! He's going to—"

"Shhh." She put a finger to my lips. "Don't believe everything you see. That image is from an hour ago. Sandra is long gone from here."

I started to laugh and tear up at the same time. I had a million questions, starting with: "H-How did you find me?"

She smiled. "Remember exiting the elevator in your building earlier tonight and bumping into an old woman carrying a bag of groceries? That was me. I planted a chip on you. It's not only a tracking device, it doubles as a mike. We now have all the self-incriminating evidence needed—Khalid Yassin's confession—to put him away for a very long..."

The door burst open, just as Lisa was untying the last strap on my right arm.

Yassin stood in the doorway with the machete in hand. He jerked backwards when he saw Lisa, then winged the weapon at her.

Lisa instantly ducked low and used a sweeping karate kick to knock the spinning machete sideways, away from herself and me.

Yassin crouched, lifted up his cuff, extracted a handgun from an ankle holster, and came up shooting.

"Get down!" Lisa hollered and gave me a shove. I toppled onto the floor just as she drew her service weapon and fired back.

They exchanged gunfire. Yassin ducked in and out of the doorway and squeezed off more shots. Lisa and I were partially protected by the table. Lisa's next bullet hit the doorframe mere inches from Yassin's head. That did it. He took off running.

It was only when Lisa heard his footsteps disappearing that she finally lowered her weapon.

I stood on legs so weak it felt like they couldn't support my weight. Lisa had said that Sandra was safe. All that mattered now was getting out alive. I turned to Lisa, told her that Yassin had a crew, any number of which could be waiting for us either in the house or outside.

She took the lead. We were bending low, while Lisa kept one hand on my shoulder, the other with the gun zigzagging left and right.

It was slow going as we made our way to the front of the house. So far, so good. Lisa opened the door. I could see her truck parked in the driveway and pointing toward the street.

"When I say *move*," she said, "that means run like hell."

I peered out, but couldn't see anyone.

"Move!" Lisa said in a whisper-shout, and we took off.

We were three or four yards away from the truck when gunfire erupted from the far corner of the house. A bullet hit the driver-side door. Lisa fired back and led the way around to the passenger side of the vehicle. She handed me the keys and instructed me to crawl in and get into the driver's seat, but to stay low until she told me to step on it.

Lisa fired three shots to give me cover. One shot was returned. As I ducked low and got into the cab, I heard her fire one more round. Then silence. Seconds later, she half-slid, half-crawled in and slammed her door shut.

"Drive!" she barked.

I straightened up in the driver's seat and saw a body on the ground. It was "Agent Atkins," the driver—probably dead.

I dropped the F-150 into gear and peeled out, making a hard right leaving the driveway, and another at the first intersection I came to.

"I think we're clear," I said. "I ... don't know what I would've done without you, Lisa. You saved me. Saved my daughter. I'm so sorry I didn't trust you. But I'll make it up to you. I swear I will. Disguising yourself and planting that chip on me was pure genius. How did you think of it? *When* did you think of it? I'm—"

She remained still. I was about to say something stupid, like: *Cat got your tongue?* when what looked like a SWAT team truck flashed past. I had no doubt it was en route to the house we'd just left.

"Lisa?"

Still nothing.

I glanced her way.

Her eyes were glazed over and there was blood oozing from her chest.

I reached a hand to her throat and could barely detect a pulse.

I sped up. The area we were approaching was familiar. I knew the location of a hospital and drove as fast as I dared.

"Don't die on me, Lisa!" I pleaded. "Please..."

EPILOGUE

I didn't make it to my condo until the light of day. Lisa had survived the three-hour operation, though she'd lost so much blood the doctors gave her chance of survival at fifty-fifty.

Jeremy had just arrived in town and was still at the hospital. He promised I'd be reunited with my daughter later this morning and sent me on ahead to shower, shave, and change into fresh clothes.

We'd briefly discussed the clue he left for me in the shipping document and how it saved me from doing something reckless. Then we'd talked about Lisa.

"She has to pull through," I said.

Jeremy studied my face and I could tell he knew how deep my feelings ran; that I was in love with her.

It was now thirty minutes past the time I expected him to show up. I was just about ready to send a text to ask where he was, when he reached me through the intercom in the lobby and I buzzed him in.

"Well?" I asked the minute he walked through the door.

He looked as tired as I felt. "She's still in a coma. Still on life support. Her primary doctor promised to call me as soon as anything changes."

"And ... my daughter?"

"Rena will be bringing her here..." he glanced at his watch, "any minute now."

"Who?" I was sure I'd heard wrong.

He smiled. "Rena Olsen's real name is Fatima Zaman. She's the girlfriend of Nassar Camir, the leader of a rival faction to Yassin. It was his team that carried out surveillance on you in London and tried to off you in Tel Aviv and Montreal, all in order to foil Yassin's mission. Long story. Anyway, Rena is a computer genius. She was able to steal the password to Sandra's room and absconded with her while Yassin was monitoring the explosions that never happened. Rena also programmed Yassin's computer to show a continuous loop of your daughter from an earlier time. No matter when he checked, he would see her tied up in the chair."

I was astounded. *Rena is a good guy? Who would-a thought?*

"How did you pull it off?" I asked. "Discover that the Zap-wireds were rigged, and find a way to disarm them?"

"Rena was keeping Camir informed whenever she could. She didn't know what Yassin's endgame was ... at first. Yassin was paranoid—or maybe just smartly cautious—and informed his various team members on a need-to-know basis. By the time Rena found out about the rigged Zapwireds, most of them had already been armed. Camir and I had crossed paths before. We called a truce to achieve a common goal: to stop Yassin. Together, we raided the SI factory and took the workers into custody. I ironed out an immunity deal with Randy Altman, aka Rayan Amin. He would continue to make his regular reports to Yassin, assuring him that even though it was a tight schedule, everything was proceeding as planned. Meanwhile, Camir's men began to carefully remove the NC-5 from the product."

I shook my head. "I can't believe you got terrorists to co-operate."

Jeremy shot me a sly look. "Well, terrorists will always be terrorists. After the NC-5 was collected and put into an underground bunker for safekeeping, I discovered about five percent was unac-counted for. While doing an inventory, it was determined that the five percent had been replaced by a gel that resembled NC-5—but was just that: a harmless gel. So much for our truce. Now I have to worry about what Camir is going to do with it."

We were about done with the coffee I'd made for both of us, when I asked Jeremy, "What about Yassin? Has he been arrested? Is he in jail?"

Jeremy turned sullen. "A few of Yassin's accomplices, Abdul Masri, Yousef Fayed, and Omar Aziz—the actors who operated the drones—were taken into custody at JFK. Yassin, I'm sorry to say, is in the wind."

"How did he escape?"

"There was a large storage shed about twenty yards behind the house with a door that opened to an alley. From the tire's skid marks it looks like he kept a motorcycle in there. All he had to do was run to the shed, fire up the bike, and take off. Probably took him 30 seconds, tops. I'll give him this—the guy planned for every eventuality."

I asked the question that had been on my mind for quite some time. "So, *who* do you and Lisa work for?"

Jeremy shrugged. "You don't give up, do you? Well, this is as much as I can tell you: There's a clandestine agency within Mossad. Ironically, it's similar to what Dalton... Yassin, that is, claimed BIS was. We work with the CIA, and occasionally the FBI, on matters between our two countries that must be kept out of the news."

The apartment intercom sounded.

"That'll be Rena and Sandra," Jeremy said.

I buzzed them in, but instead of waiting, I stepped into the hallway, hardly able to stand still.

The elevator door no sooner opened when I heard my daughter scream, "Daddy!" and she came rushing toward me.

Her embrace nearly bowled me over.

I was on my knees, holding on to her for dear life. She started to cry and I couldn't contain my tears either.

We were headed inside my condo, when Rena turned away. "I've got a plane to catch," she said. "I'm—uh—sorry for the way I treated you, Blair. But, as you can appreciate, I had to be convincing."

I watched her go, still finding it difficult to compartmentalize her involvement.

Before we sat down, I asked Sandra if she was hungry.

"Not really," she said. "But can I have a glass of milk?'

It was a mundane thing, but for some reason it nearly brought me to tears again.

"You have a seat in the den," I said. "Put on the TV. I'll bring it in to you."

Jeremy followed me into the kitchen and I thanked him profusely for helping save both mine and my daughter's life. "But why didn't you get to us sooner?" I asked. "If you had arrested Yassin, Lisa never would've been shot."

He let out a deep sigh. "It was Lisa's idea to wait. She argued that if we could get Yassin to confess his plan for mass homicide on tape, it would be solid evidence to convict him of terrorist insurgency against the US, and ensure he didn't get off on some loophole."

"And you went along with her?"

"Of course, I went along. As you know, my flight was delayed. But Lisa and I were communicating by text. She had no choice but to handle this on her own."

"Despite the risk?"

"I tried to dissuade her. She wouldn't take no for an answer. She knew Yassin would go ballistic once he found out his plan was thwarted."

This made sense, but still I was upset. "Wasn't there another way?"

"Think about it, Blair. When the Zapwired product arrived on American soil they were no longer armed, so no crime there."

"Yassin murdered Mandy, Frank, and some poor runaway girl."

"You and I know that. But the investigators ruled it an accident. Lisa gambled correctly that Yassin would not be able to resist bragging about his master plan to you. And now, thanks to her, and the chip she planted on you, we have his confession on tape."

My voice rose. "But Yassin got away."

"So far."

Jeremy's cell phone buzzed. He said hello and listened. Then his face became ashen.

I forced myself to ask, "L-Lisa?"

"Blair ... we've got to get to the hospital right away."

*

It was a blur, so I couldn't honestly say how the three of us got there as fast as we did. Sandra, understandably, wanted to stay glued to my side. I did my best to reassure her that the trauma she went through was over, and there was nothing to worry about.

The head nurse, Emily Robinson, immediately arranged for a place where my daughter could wait for us—a semi-private room equipped with children's story books and a television. Then, she assigned a cheerful young nurse to stay with her.

Nurse Robinson led Jeremy and me into her office, which was hardly bigger than a cubbyhole, with barely enough room for her desk and two metal bridge chairs opposite.

The woman looked like a sophisticated version of the prototypical grandmother: gray hair, with an abundance of wrinkles, but an erect posture and a manner so warm it would put anyone at ease.

Once Jeremy and I had settled into our seats, she didn't waste any time: "Ms. Brandt was removed from a medically-induced coma a short time ago. This is why I called you here. There is always a risk as to how it will turn out. The next little while should tell us a lot more. She's not able to talk yet. However, I can take you in to see her now, if you'd like. But I don't want you drawing any conclusions. It's still early."

I stood quicker than I intended and had to steady myself. There could be no misinterpreting the cautionary tone in the head nurse's voice. She led the way into the corridor and we followed.

But before we could get very far, a tall female orderly approached and asked to speak to Nurse Robinson alone.

It wasn't long before a pallor came over the head nurse's face. She reversed direction and led us back to her office, where we all remained standing. "We've run into a problem," she said. "Ms. Brandt lost a lot of blood. There might be permanent brain damage. More tests will have to be run. I'm afraid I must ask you to come back tomorrow morning."

Permanent brain damage? I wanted to rail against the injustice.

We said goodbye to Nurse Robinson, collected my daughter, and headed out.

Jeremy said something to me that I missed. He continued speaking but I ignored him.

"Blair?" he put a hand on my arm. "Are you okay?"

I couldn't express how I felt and hoped my shoulder shrug would suffice.

We returned to my condo where I poured a stiff Scotch for myself, a Coke for Jeremy, and orange juice for Sandra. Jeremy and I didn't want to eat but we ordered a pizza for my daughter that she seemed to enjoy. After I put Sandra to bed, I turned on the TV, then both Jeremy and I pretended to be interested in a Yankees ballgame.

My mind kept coming back to Lisa. Her bravery warranted recognition. She deserved to make a full recovery, to be able to accept every honor that could be bestowed upon her, not locked in a vegetative state for the rest of her life.

*

Jeremy made use of the spare bedroom, while I spent the night contemplating every possibility that would face us in the morning. I understood it was out of my hands but I willed my opinion to count, to force my desire to mean something and push the odds in Lisa's favor.

At 8:00 a.m. I picked up the house phone and called my neighbor. Mila Harris was a sixty-two-year-old widow I'd befriended over the years. She'd babysat for my daughter in the past and I was hoping she could do so now. I apologized for calling so early and asked if she was available.

"Not early at all," she said, "and I'm available but not cheap."

I forced a chuckle to show I appreciated her sense of humor. "I'll bring her over in about a half hour," I said, "if that's okay with you?"

"A half hour is fine."

I hung up, quickly showered and shaved. When I came out of the bathroom, I found Jeremy had already served Sandra breakfast, so she was ready to go.

"Can I get you something?" my friend asked.

I declined, anxious to leave for the hospital.

*

We arrived at the reception desk and were told to wait. It was only a few minutes, but it felt like forever before Nurse Robinson finally came bounding up from her office and asked us to follow her. I hoped her upbeat mood was a good sign, but didn't want to jinx it by asking if Lisa was okay.

She led the way along the corridor and into a front room in the ICU. The lights were dimmed, the monitoring machines had been turned off, and the bed was ... empty.

I could read the surprise on the head nurse's face and fear seized my gut. *No, no, no!* Lisa not being here could only mean one thing.

"Stay where you are," Nurse Robinson instructed, then she hurried out of the room.

I glanced at Jeremy and could tell he was thinking the same thing.

It was difficult not to monitor the time, which was all I did, until I heard a familiar voice approaching, and my heart didn't just skip a beat, it felt as if it might gallop out of my chest.

"H-Hello ... b-boys," a drowsy-looking Lisa managed in a frail whisper.

Nurse Robinson was beaming as she pushed the wheel chair into the room. "Sorry, no one told me, but she was off for more X-rays."

Both Jeremy and I started talking at once.

"Easy," Nurse Robinson cautioned as she helped Lisa out of the wheel chair and into the bed. "She's still quite weak."

I had an immediate question, but the head nurse answered before it could be asked. "Baring anything unforeseen," she said, "Ms. Brandt should make a full recovery." She paused. "Now... you have five minutes, then I want you both out of here. Our patient needs her rest."

*

I let Jeremy monopolize what little there was of the conversation. He needed to get some specific operational details from Lisa in the short time we had. However, it didn't take long before Lisa began to drift off, and we both got up to leave.

Jeremy had to get back in Israel, and I drove him to the airport the next morning. From there I went to the hospital, only to find visitors were not allowed until later in the day.

Rather than stick around, I figured my time would best be served at work. It felt like ages since I'd last been in the office, especially when my secretary greeted me like a conquering hero.

"I want to know everything," she said, parking herself in front of my desk.

"Nora—it's complicated. Give me a few days. Okay? Then I'll treat you to lunch."

"Promise?"

"Yes."

Once alone, I went through the pile of memos and correspondence on my desk, wondering who it was that said we now operated in a paperless work environment.

There were letters to be answered and contracts to be signed. But most important were the Zapwired sales reports. Each of the five New York boroughs showed similar results—a complete sellout! I knew not to get ahead of myself, though it was tough not to.

The buyers from each retailer who'd participated in the launch were not only unanimously proclaiming the game an unqualified hit, they now insisted on placing rollout orders for their stores across America. I tallied their purchases and found them so aggressive, I had to do a recount. The totals matched! Numbers don't lie: Zapwired was headed for stardom; rivaling, maybe even exceeding Nintendo's Game Boy.

It would've been nice to sit back for a while and bask in my success, but when I checked my watch it was mid-afternoon; time to return to the hospital.

Lisa made an effort to smile when she saw me, though it was a difficult undertaking. She still wasn't herself and I knew I had to be patient. Before long I was advised by a nurse that visiting-hours were over.

Toward the end of the week, to my great relief, a bit of Lisa's spark had returned. But she reminded me that Jeremy had insisted she must get back to Israel as soon as possible for a debriefing at Headquarters.

"Ah," I said, "the, uh, outfit that has no name."

She hid her amusement well. "That one."

"So—will I ever see you again?"

"Hmm," she contemplated, more to herself, "I have paid leave coming up in three-month's time..."

I didn't hesitate, asking hopefully, "And you'll spend it here, in New York, with me?"

She frowned. "What makes you say that?"

"Huh?"

"Just kidding." She flashed an ear-to-ear grin. "I've already booked my flight."

ACKNOWLEDGMENTS

I will forever be indebted to my editor, Cliff Carle, whose vision and guidance make me a far better writer. I thank him for his time and special talent.

I want to express my appreciation for my Publisher, Tracy Ertl, who remains a special friend and deserves a clean bill of health.

And to my wife, Francine, a woman whose selflessness is beyond measure. Thank you for continuing to put up with me. You deserve far more than a medal.